You are cordially invited to the wedding

of

Jack Keaton and Stephanie Brewster

at the

Paradise Hotel,

Hawaii

The bride and groom will not be attending.
In their place, the matron of honor,
Bentley Brewster DeHaven,
and her husband, Carter DeHaven,
will renew their vows.

In the event that Carter doesn't actually
exist, Mitch Slater
has kindly consented to stand in as tthe groom.

Please join us for this joyful occasion.
We are assured that the weather reports
are greatly exaggerated.

Dear Reader,

We're so glad you could join us in beautiful Hawaii for what promises to be another perfect wedding! But wait—let's hear it from the mother-of-the-bride herself, Babs Brewster:

"As if it's not bad enough that Stephanie is missing her wedding, now my *other* daughter is driving me crazy. Bentley's got everything a girl could ask for, and is she happy? No! She isn't the least bit grateful for her wonderful husband—at least he *sounds* wonderful. We haven't met him, or seen pictures of him...and how long do I have to wait for a grandchild? And if that's not enough to worry about, there's the hurricane and we'll probably all be washed out to sea! I ask you, what's a mother to do?"

You're about to find out as we bring you the second of THREE WEDDINGS & A HURRICANE, a hilarious new trilogy from friends Debbi Rawlins, Jo Leigh and Karen Toller Whittenburg. Be sure you don't miss out on a single minute of the fun. Watch for the next book—*Please Say "I Do"*—coming to you next month.

Happy reading!

Debra Matteucci
Senior Editor & Editorial Coordinator
Harlequin Books
300 East 42nd Street
New York, NY 10017

QUICK, FIND A RING!

Jo Leigh

Harlequin Books

TORONTO • NEW YORK • LONDON
AMSTERDAM • PARIS • SYDNEY • HAMBURG
STOCKHOLM • ATHENS • TOKYO • MILAN
MADRID • WARSAW • BUDAPEST • AUCKLAND

This book would not have happened without the wondrous and talented Debbi Quattrone and Karen Crane. You two made it more fun than it had any right to be. Special thanks to Bonnie Crisalli for bringing me into the fold, Huntley Fitzpatrick for her astute editing and kindness, and Debra Matteucci for giving the green light.

ISBN 0-373-16695-8

QUICK, FIND A RING!

Prologue

Mitch Slater quietly checked the area around his desk. Bob Gleeson sat hunched over his computer, his back so curved he looked like a gargoyle. Natch talked on the phone while he tried to look up Loreen Firestone's skirt. Three or four copy boys scurried around the office like mice in a maze. Jerry's editor screamed bloody murder about a typo.

It was a little on the quiet side, but all in all, just a typical morning at the *Times*. No one was paying any attention to him, so he quickly opened the Calendar section and read his horoscope.

Nothing to write home about. Just that he should take his Capricorn butt on a vacation, where, according to the stars, he would find true love. Like that was a possibility.

He folded the paper, checking once more to see if he'd been caught, but another day had begun with his secret vice intact. That alone should have made him happy, but it didn't.

Darren Colker was too much on his mind. And of

course, Bentley. Despite her protestations, he knew damn well she was trying to scoop him on the Colker interview. It was too juicy a piece for her to let it go. She was champing at the bit to get her hands on the most reclusive capitalist since Howard Hughes. His fortune had been estimated at over seventy billion—with a capital B—and he hadn't been seen in more than ten months. Many speculated that he was dead. Mitch didn't buy it. Colker was alive. Just hiding. In Hawaii.

At least that was his guess. More than a guess. Just not a fact. If his luck continued to run, he'd get the true skinny in the next couple of days. A few well-placed phone calls and a little bribe dough would work the magic. Then he'd know for sure.

Right now, though, he had an expense report to file. He searched the chaos that was his desk, but no form appeared. He looked over at Bentley's desk. Neat beyond the endurance of most sentient beings, she would have a form. He knew that without question. She would have twelve, one for each month. They would be in a separate file and they would each be marked with little white tabs. It gave him the willies.

Supposedly, she was running some personal errands. Yeah. Like she had to run her own errands. Her husband, the fabulous Carter DeHaven, made sure she didn't want for anything. Maids, cars, golden credit cards. The woman had it made in the shade with Rich Boy. Of course she had time to dig around about Colker.

Mitch went over to her desk. He picked up the fancy little nameplate she was so fond of. Bentley DeHaven. The name sounded like something from a comic strip. Actually, she did sort of remind him of Brenda Starr, only with blond hair. Proportioned to kill, with those long Barbie legs. Just the kind of babe that would look great in his pajama tops. Pity he couldn't stand her.

He leaned back against the side of the desk and slid the front drawer open. She'd warned him to stay away from her stuff. More than once. But surely even Bentley wouldn't begrudge him a little form, would she? He opened the drawer wider.

When the coast was clear, he glanced down. Nothing, nothing. Wait. An airline ticket. Throwing caution to the wind, he turned and yanked the folded paper out, opening it so quickly the crease tore.

Hawaii.

He *knew* it. Damn it. She'd found Colker. Her flight was leaving tomorrow. Six days. Paradise Bay Honeymoon Hotel? Clever. Colker was hiding in a honeymoon hotel, the last place anyone would look. How had Bentley found him?

It didn't matter. He picked up her phone and called the American Airlines 800 number.

"When's your next flight to Hawaii?"

While the reservations clerk looked that up, Mitch glanced once more at the ticket, only then noticing the yellow paper inside the folder. Her itinerary no doubt. He pulled it loose. And read.

He stopped breathing. His pulse quickened. This

was no itinerary. This was dynamite. Nitroglycerin. Better than his wildest dreams!

He folded the paper up, stuck it in place, then slipped the whole enchilada back into her desk.

Mrs. Bentley DeHaven was in for a little surprise.

No one got the best of Mitch Slater. Not even for a lei.

Chapter One

Bentley checked her mascara in her small mirror. Travel didn't agree with her—especially when her destination was so perilous. It was the first time in nearly three years she was going to face her entire family. Including Aunt Tildy. And, of course, there was the lie.

She tried to patch up what she could on her face, then gave it up and put the mirror in her purse. There was a much more pressing matter.

She'd rehearsed it all the way across the Pacific. "No, Mother, Carter couldn't be here. Of course he wanted to come. It's his job." It sounded so phony. Anyone with a lick of intelligence would spot it for a fabrication. A prevarication. A big fat whopper. But what else could she do? Carter DeHaven had saved her sanity. He'd rescued her from endless dates, blind and otherwise, all hideous.

Her mother's only passion, the one thing she felt was her real calling, was making "appropriate" matches for her relatives, particularly her children.

As the eldest daughter, Bentley had suffered through the Coming Out Process, the Sorority Process, the Church as Heavenly Place to Find a Mate Process, the Your Mother Called My Mother Process and infinite varieties of the torture known as Snagging a Catch.

In her case, a "catch" was quite specific. Blue of blood, thick of wallet and more reactionary than conservative. Personality? Immaterial. Ambition? Just enough to keep the status quo. The ultimate goal? To produce heirs, so that the entire process could be repeated over and over until the inbreeding created a race entirely separate from the rest of humanity. *Homo Neiman-Marcus.* He who shops erect.

But Carter didn't need heirs. Which was the only part of Carter that didn't fit the bill. He was himself an heir, richer than John-John Kennedy but not as rich as Bob Hope. He was gorgeous—not as gorgeous as John-John but *nothing* like Hope, thank you. And, more important than any other single thing about him—he left her alone. Entirely alone. Bless his little Republican heart.

She'd made a promise to herself on the day she'd married Carter. No matter what it took, she was going to win a Pulitzer prize for journalism before she turned thirty-five. Nothing, not even a husband, especially not a husband, was going to stand in her way.

It didn't hurt that Darren Colker was rumored to be in Hawaii. As long as she was there for her sister's wedding, she might as well dig around. Wouldn't that just steam Mitch's coffee. She'd get the interview of a lifetime, and he'd choke on every word. It had been tricky, not letting on about the wedding, but she'd pulled it off. If she could only pull things off with her family, then everything would be just fine.

She closed the small window, leaned her head on the tiny airline pillow and closed her eyes. Visions of Mitch tearing his hair out helped her drift into a blissful sleep.

THE HOTEL WAS a picture postcard come to life. White, huge, airy and lush, it was Fantasy Island, Bali Hai. Even the walk to the front desk was filled with luscious smells and exotic sounds. The foliage was primordial, the air soft and moist against her skin. Her sister sure had taste. What a place to tie the knot.

It wasn't traditional, especially not for her family, but she'd known Stephanie's fiancé, Jack, most of her life, and for him, this was a perfect setting. He was more accustomed to the Amazon, where he was a safari guide, but when called upon, the boy could relax in luxury with the best of them. It would be nice seeing him again, assuming she had a chance.

She hadn't had time to discuss this wedding with Steph, but her instincts told her that her baby sister was marrying Jack for the same reason she had married Carter. Good for her.

At the busy front desk, she waited for two honeymoon couples to check in, wishing they'd stop the giggling and smooching and get down to business. She was tired, and she wanted a shower.

"You have a reservation for Bentley DeHaven," she said as soon as the desk clerk smiled her way.

He was tall, young and dressed in a floral shirt that might lead to astigmatism if looked at too long. But he was friendly and efficient, and the checking in was handled quickly. He handed her the electronic key and gave her directions to her room, then rang for a bellman.

"Can you tell me if Stephanie Brewster has checked in yet?"

The young man hit his keyboard a few times. "Not yet."

"What about Danforth and Babs Brewster?"

He pressed one key. "That's right. I thought I remembered that party. They arrived yesterday. Quite a large group, I recall."

"Yes, I imagine it was."

He smiled at her, not acknowledging the sigh in her voice or the pain in her eyes. His gaze shifted and she turned to the bellman. This one was young, too, although he was beefy and dark. Native looking. Very handsome. His gold nameplate read Kimo, and he smiled with startling white teeth as he gathered her luggage.

"I'll take these up for you, miss."

She nodded.

He led the way to the elevator, and she caught a glimpse of a waterfall with a pool-bar to her right. It was a large bar, covered with a sort of thatched, Tikiroom-looking thing so that the daily rain squalls wouldn't interrupt the romance between blended liquor and vacationers. The tiny-umbrella business was alive and well here at the Paradise Bay Honeymoon Hotel. Oh, yes.

Kimo smiled again as she entered the elevator. "There's a storm coming, miss," he said. "Might be a big one."

"Oh?"

"It's already blowing on some of the outer islands."

"Will it affect the hotel?"

"Never can tell, miss. It might."

"Swell."

"Those, too. Big ones. Don't want to be caught in a boat when the hurricanes come."

She smiled. "I'll remember that, thank you."

"My pleasure."

The elevator stopped on the fourteenth floor, and Kimo led her down a green-carpeted hallway to room 1457. He opened the door and let her enter before he brought her bags in.

It was a lovely room. One wall had two big windows, and the view took her breath away. The ocean, dark blue against the roiling sky above it, sparkled with light and whitecaps. There were several sailboats dashing across the waves, despite Kimo's warning, and some brave soul tethered to a sail was flying behind a speedboat.

"The bathroom is in here, miss," Kimo said, snatching her attention from the parasailor.

She followed him to the large bath, which had a stall shower and a heart-shaped Jacuzzi tub. The commode was judiciously hidden behind a half wall, and there was a double-sink vanity.

The room decor was light, lots of beautiful pastels and palm leaves. Kimo showed her the spacious closet, the king-size bed, the television and, of course, the honor bar. It would be easy to relax here, to forget Los Angeles, the *Times* and Mitch. She hadn't had a real vacation in about three years, and this just might be the ticket. That is, if Mother let her alone.

She gave Kimo a nice tip, and he left her with another dazzling smile. Then, although she should unpack, she took out her airline ticket and opened the folder. She pulled her little yellow note out of the side and read it one more time. Then she tore the only tangible evidence of her secret into little bitty pieces and dropped them like confetti into the toilet. She smiled as she flushed. All was right with the world.

BABS BREWSTER ANNOUNCED her presence with the jangle of a dozen bracelets. Bentley had a flash of a jungle movie she'd seen long ago, where the natives beat on drums to flush tigers out of the bushes. Smart tigers ran like hell. She smiled at her mother.

"Bentley, my darling, it's been so long I hardly recognized you."

"Hello, Mother." A couple of air kisses near each

cheek signaled the emotional peak of the day. "You look great, as always."

She did, too. Babs subsidized the entire plastic surgery business in the Boston area, all by herself. She was a master sculpture, and except for that not being able to blink all the way thing, she was gorgeous. Someone had once told her that she looked like Joan Kennedy before the Bad Times, and Babs had made it her life's business to promote the idea. Her hair was shoulder length, blond courtesy of Clairol, and as her crowd would say, "sharp." Her clothes were nothing but Givenchy or Lauren, no exceptions. Today it was white capri pants, a white T-shirt that must have cost more than two hundred dollars and a whimsically bright sash around her emaciated waist. Babs was ever ready for the Condé Nast photographers.

Her mother was giving her the once-over. Bentley should have been used to it by now, but it still made her feel like a floral arrangement with too many weeds.

"That color isn't good for you, dear. Go deeper. You're winter, remember? Reds, vermilions. Bold. Brash."

"I'll be bold and brash tonight, okay?"

"Sassy already, eh?" She turned to look behind her, and Bentley saw her father round the corner from the bar. "Danny, our girl's being sassy."

"Eh? What?"

Danforth "Danny" Brewster was the ideal mate for Babs, but he was, unfortunately, no Atticus Finch.

Silver haired, handsome, slender, he looked great by
the fireplace with a pipe in one hand. Today, he was
in his sailor outfit, which he wore quite often back
home, although to Bentley's knowledge, he'd never
actually sailed in his life. But Babs said the hat
worked.

"I said," Babs fairly shouted, "that Bentley is being sassy." Then she leaned toward her and whispered, "The hearing aid cost a small fortune, and
he's still deaf as a post."

"Bentley, girl. Let me look at you."

She smiled at her father and watched in dismay as
more of her relatives oozed from the bar to the lobby.
Aunt Tildy with her cane, Uncle Arthur with his hideous toupee. Cousins, nephews, nieces. And that
wasn't all of them.

"So," Babs said, loudly enough for Danny, and
the rest of the world, to hear. "Where is he? We're
all dying to meet your Carter, darling. I can't believe
I've never even seen my own son-in-law. I mean,
really."

Bentley opened her mouth, ready with the speech
she'd practiced a hundred times. But she didn't say
a word. She just made a small choking sound.

Because just then, Mitch Slater appeared out of
nowhere, stepped up to Babs Brewster and said,
"I'm right here, Mother."

Chapter Two

Mitch hadn't had this much fun since he'd put the pigs in the principal's office in high school. Just the look on Bentley's face would give him good memories into his dotage. For a moment he thought she might faint, but hey, you can't have everything.

"So this is the famous Carter?" Bentley's mother said, eyeing him like a tennis bracelet. "You didn't tell us he was this beautiful, Bentley. Oh, the children are going to be stunning!"

Mitch smiled at Mom, then turned again to Bentley. "We're going to work on that while we're here, aren't we, sweetheart?"

Bentley's mouth opened, but nothing came out. Her face was an odd shade of pink, though. And getting brighter by the moment.

"Let me shake your hand, son," Bentley's father said. Mitch recognized him from newspaper photographs, same thing with Babs. He knew Bentley came from old money, from people who made the social registry on a regular basis. So he'd done his homework before getting on the plane. He'd rented three Katharine Hepburn movies and watched them as he'd packed. It didn't go past him that Carter DeHaven was damn similar to C. K. Dexter Haven, the Cary Grant role in *The Philadelphia Story.* Bentley had been clever, but not clever enough.

"It's good to finally meet you, sir," Mitch said. "I've been remiss. I should have made it a point to do this sooner."

"Well, I'm just pleased as punch we can be together for this wonderful occasion. Why don't we go to the bar? Let your old man buy you a drink."

He glanced at Bentley. Her color was better, but her shock was quickly shifting into anger. "Great idea, sir." He put his hand on the small of Babs's back. "After you, Mother. I want to meet the family. Snookems has told me so much about all of you." He smiled at his bride. "Haven't you, snookems?"

"I'll give you snookems—"

Mitch sidestepped Bentley and walked quickly toward the bar, sandwiched between Babs and Danny Brewster.

Bentley didn't move. She couldn't. She'd been turned to stone by the evil warlock Mitch who'd come to Hawaii to ruin her life. How the hell had he known Carter didn't exist? She'd never been more careful with anything in her life. She'd covered her tracks so well the CIA wouldn't have been able to find a shred of evidence.

Carter had given her great pleasure. He'd offered

her solace in a crazy world. Laughter in her most bitter moments. And now he was gone. There was only one solution. Widowhood. Soon.

For the first time since Mitch had shown up, she smiled. Planning his demise softened the blow somewhat, at least enough to get her moving. She couldn't leave Mitch alone with her family. God knows what he'd say. She thought of him calling her snookems and eliminated poison as too kind a murder weapon. She was in Hawaii—why not throw him into a volcano?

The family was spread out in the bar, closer to the liquor than the waterfall. Mitch was center stage, sitting next to her parents. Everyone smiled jauntily, as if this were a vacation or something. Mitch grinned at her and patted the seat next to his. She came up behind him.

"Sit down, honey," he said. "Mother was just saying that we should come out to the house this winter for the holidays. I agree, don't you?"

"We'll see, *dear*." As she sat, she reached under the small table and pinched his thigh as hard as she could.

"Ouch." Mitch grabbed her hand and held it tightly. Very tightly.

"What's wrong, son?" Dan said, signaling the waiter.

"Old war injury."

"The war's just started," Bentley whispered, struggling to get her hand back.

Mitch leaned close to her, still keeping her hand in his. "Darling, you wouldn't want your family to see us fight, would you? You don't want them knowing our *secrets*."

"Order champagne, Danny," Babs said. "We need to toast Carter. We didn't get to at the wedding."

"Of course." Dan turned to the waiter and made the request. "Five bottles ought to do it."

Bentley pulled her hand out of Mitch's grasp, nearly tilting in her chair with the effort. She grabbed the end of the waiter's shirt, stopping him. "Scotch," she said. "A double. And three aspirin."

He nodded, and she turned just in time to see Mitch give her mother a patronizing, commiserating eye-roll. That did it. The volcano was too good for him. She'd find an anthill and stake him out naked in the sun. Then she'd dribble honey all over his—

"Your work sounds fascinating," Babs said. "But so dangerous."

Bentley froze. What if he told her family a completely different story from the one she'd made up? Everything could come apart at the seams.

"Working for CNN had its moments. But…" He gave her an angelic smile. "I was going to save this surprise until we were alone, but it's just so darn great to be with all our loved ones, I'll tell you now."

Bentley was glad she'd updated her will before the trip. Because she was clearly having a heart attack.

That must be his plan. This whole thing was a plot to kill her.

"Snookems," he said, "I've given notice. I'm coming back to L.A. for good. We can finally start our family."

The champagne arrived just then. Three waiters put down tall ice buckets, and each man popped a cork.

"Divine timing." Babs held out her glass for her bubbly. "This does require a toast. You know we want nothing more than a grandchild, isn't that right, Danny?"

"That's right, Babs. An heir. A grandson."

Glasses were filled at all the small tables, with the last two flutes belonging to Mitch and Bentley. Dan stood and held his glass aloft. "To our new son, and the sons he will have. To Carter!"

Dan drank, Babs drank, Mitch drank. Bentley brought her drink under the table and poured the cold champagne directly onto her darling Carter's lap.

It did her heart good to hear his yelp. To see him leap to his feet. To hear the chair fall, the glass break, the waiter slip, the ice cascade prettily on the floor.

Then she picked up her scotch and her aspirin. She swallowed all three tablets while waiter number two slid on the ice and fell into Aunt Tildy's lap. Her shriek shook the rafters, but her cane did the real damage. She knocked over another ice bucket, then hit Uncle Arthur in the stomach on the follow-through. He bent double, and his toupee fell onto the icy floor, looking something like a dead wolverine.

Bentley sipped again as Babs shot into the air, causing her own champagne to spray all over Dan's sailor suit. Dan, in turn, stood up to help Babs but slipped in the ice and slid down, rather elegantly, to the floor, hanging on to Babs's capri pants.

Mitch, she noticed, had taken his seat once more. He scooted close to her and put his arm on the back of her chair. "Good," he said. "Excellent. You have a real talent for this."

"Thank you."

"So, we're even, right?"

"Oh my, no. We won't be even until you're dead."

"Ah. I see."

"Good. I don't want you to be surprised. I know *I* hate surprises."

"I wouldn't have had to surprise you if you'd told me you were going after Colker."

"Does this look like I'm here on a story?"

"Yeah. Uh-huh. Colker's in Hawaii, you're in Hawaii. Big coincidence."

"Believe what you want."

"We already know just how good a liar you are, Mrs. DeHaven."

"Oh, the ways I'm going to pay you back for this are going to make headlines."

"Uh, uh, uh, snookems. All I have to do is blow

the whistle, and your master plan goes right into the toilet.''

"My master plan?''

"Yeah. I'm sure Babs and Dan would love to know that not only am I not Carter, but Carter is a figment of your imagination. That darling Bentley has been lying to Mommy and Daddy all this time. Might put a chink in the old trust fund, eh?''

"You're as insane as you are dangerous.''

"Maybe so. But it doesn't matter. I've got you over a barrel, honey lamb, and don't you forget it.''

"So what do you want?''

"Everything you know about Colker.''

"That's easy. Nothing.''

He shook his head. "Bentley, you might be able to fool your parents, but don't try it on me.''

"Oh, you can tell when I'm lying, huh?''

"In a second.''

"So you've known the whole time that I wasn't married?''

"Of course.''

"I'm going to pick up my father now. You may go to hell.''

She stood up and carefully made her way through the ice patches to where Dan sat. She gave him her hand, and he stood. At first she thought he was crying, but then she looked at his face. He was hysterical. He was laughing harder than she'd ever seen him laugh before. "Did you see,'' he said, trying to keep it together long enough to talk, "did you see the toupee?"

She nodded, seeing nothing amusing in the circumstance. Was Mitch telling the truth? Had he known from the beginning?

"Did you hear Tildy? The old bat hasn't been this alive in forty years."

Bentley smiled, although not for long. All her satisfaction at dumping her drink on Mitch had fled, and she didn't even get the pleasure of seeing her parents angry at him for causing a scene. It wasn't fair. Even Babs was managing to keep her cool. She had her compact in one hand and a hairbrush in the other.

Bentley left Dan and Babs and moved over to Uncle Arthur, who was trying to put his toupee back on. He didn't seem to know which end was the front, so she helped, although his rug was a bit worse for wear. He was grateful for her help, though, and she felt a pang of guilt. Not just for him, but for the poor waiters. No, it wasn't her fault. It was *Mitch.* He was the devil. And he must be stopped.

MITCH THOUGHT ABOUT going upstairs to change. But he didn't know Bentley's room number, and he didn't have a key. So he watched her settle her uncle's toupee on his head. The nerve of her trying to tell him she wasn't on Colker's trail. Well, he held all the cards in this game. Playing Carter was actually kind of fun. He liked the way her family treated him. Hell, they treated him better than they treated her.

Maybe that was normal. He wouldn't know. He tried to imagine his own mother here, but he couldn't. They probably wouldn't have let her into the hotel.

He shook that thought off and concentrated again on Bentley. It was clear she was going to try to get back at him. So he was going to have to be particularly clever. Watch his every move. The good news was the ace he held. She'd have to behave. At least in public.

She bent over a table to pick up an ice bucket, and Mitch got a look at her legs and derriere. It was all he could do not to applaud. How could someone so manipulative live in a body that sweet? Despite the fact that she was the most annoying woman he'd ever met, he couldn't deny the fact that she was gorgeous. One thing money had given her was taste. He'd never seen her look anything but spectacular. Even when she'd gone downtown to chase a story, she dressed like a queen.

He liked what she had on now. Simple tailored pink slacks and a white blouse. Nothing special. Just perfect. He'd always figured he'd like what was underneath her clothes, and hot-diggity, this just might be his chance to find out for sure.

Then she turned to face him, and his excitement dwindled. He seriously doubted she'd be up for snuggling tonight. She just had no sense of humor.

"What are you looking at?"

"Nothing."

"Well, keep it that way."

"Yes, dear."

She approached. He couldn't help but notice her hands were now fists. And that she looked as though she knew how to use them. This was a whole new side of Bentley. A new dangerous side. He stood and inched his way toward Babs. Bentley wouldn't hit him in front of Mommy, now would she?

"Anyone else hungry?" he said, hoping someone would take the bait. It was early yet, but he needed the family to stick around. It was safer that way.

"It's only four-thirty," Babs said. "Darlings, we're going up to the room. We're both a mess."

"No!" Mitch swung to his "mother" and grasped her arms. "Don't go."

Babs reached up and pinched his cheek. "Isn't that sweet? Danny, look how sweet. Bentley, you didn't tell me he'd be this sweet."

"Sweet?"

Bentley's voice had a disturbing edge to it. Slightly psychopathic.

"Oh, he's a doll. A peach. A real cupcake."

"Bentley…"

"What is it, snookems?" she said as if butter wouldn't melt in her mouth. "Don't you want to go up to the room with me so we can *rest?*"

"Me? Nah. I'm not tired."

"But you need to change clothes, Carter."

He laughed, sort of. "No, no. I'm fine. I'll just stay down here."

Bentley smiled at him then. It made his blood flow cold.

"I *need* you to come upstairs with me, Carter."

He backed up until his butt hit a table. He checked for an escape route, but he figured he'd have to jump over Uncle Arthur to make a clean getaway, and the old man might not make it.

A change in tactics was definitely in order.

He walked toward Bentley, remembering who was who and what was what. He'd never been afraid of a woman in his life, and he wasn't about to start now.

He grabbed her around the middle and pulled her close. He laughed at the look of panic in her eyes. Then he kissed her, and to show who was boss, he caught her hand just as it was coming up to hit him. Then he kissed her harder.

Chapter Three

It took a minute for the nerve endings from his mouth to connect to his brain. They were clearly dazed by the fact that he was, in fact, kissing Bentley De-Haven. Not just kissing her. *Kissing* her. It had started as a closed-mouth, teeth-clenched battle of locked lips, but before he'd had a chance to consider the consequences, he'd introduced a whole different approach to the matter. It wasn't his fault. He was sure of that. His tongue got involved without his permission. It was the taste of her. The slightly sweet, delicate, one-hundred-proof softness that was so unique that he had never, would never, taste anything like it again.

The sounds of the bar, the waterfall, Babs and Dan, Aunt Tildy, all faded away to a hazy buzz. He still held Bentley's wrist in his hand, but the fight had gone out of her. He wanted to move again, to explore this new situation more fully, but he hesitated. He didn't like Bentley DeHaven. She didn't like him. But, oh, mama, this kiss was...was...

She shifted, and her tongue slipped past his teeth and tentatively tasted him in return. All higher functions in his brain shut down, boom, like that. His thoughts were primal, repetitive, simple. *Yes. Good. More.*

Another part of his body got into the act, roused by the sensations up above. He moved his hips closer to Bentley until they met thigh to thigh. Then she did it again. She moved. Just a little. Just enough. He was about to embarrass himself in front of his in-laws.

Then she broke free. She disengaged, yanked her arm from his grasp, took two steps back and gave him a look that would melt iron ore.

"You son of a—"

"Bentley," he said loudly, moving aside so she could see Mom and Dad. "We need to go to the room, honey. It's early yet. Plenty of time to get changed and freshen up."

Her gaze locked onto his, and he felt the hate vibrations scorch his corneas. He also saw that Bentley was blushing. Pink as a rose from her neck to her hairline. There was some satisfaction in that accomplishment, but not much.

"Yes," she said, the word hot as lava. "Let's go to the room. Let's freshen up."

Mitch smiled. He turned and put his arm around her shoulder. She struggled for a second, but he could bench-press two hundred and fifty pounds, so he won. Then he leaned close to her, moving his mouth right next to her ear. Babs probably would think he was nibbling her daughter's lobe, whispering sweet nothings. Ha.

"Do not," he murmured, "blow this. I'm Carter, remember? Your loving husband." Then he smiled at Babs.

"Oh, it does my heart good to see you two lovebirds together," Babs said. "I don't know when I've been happier. I just pray that Stephanie finds as much happiness as her sister. Right, Dan?"

"Huh?" Dan was still wiping his shirt with a napkin.

"I said I hope Stephanie and Jack will be as happy as Bentley and Carter."

Dan stopped wiping. "Where is she?"

"Who?"

"Stephanie."

Babs smiled indulgently, but Mitch saw the impatience behind the cheery facade. "I told you, she's supposed to arrive tomorrow. Although I've been trying to convince her to get here today. That storm isn't going away."

Dan nodded. Babs patted his hand. Aunt Tildy walked past them, her cane loud on the stone floor. Uncle Arthur, still trying to place his toupee on correctly, followed. The waiters mopped up champagne.

Bentley pulled free of Mitch's embrace. She needed to get out of there, away from her mother, her father and especially Mitch. She had to focus, to think logically, to plan her revenge.

"I'm going to the rest room. Excuse me."

Before anyone could stop her she fled, walking quickly but carefully on the wet floor, right past the palm tree into the large powder room.

She was alone. Thank goodness. Life had suddenly become a Tilt-A-Whirl and she'd lost the handrail.

The light in the powder room was soft, easy on the eyes, but she still saw her own reflection in too much detail. Her hair was a mess, her blouse disheveled, her lipstick worn off.

Her lipstick.

What in hell had happened to her when he... When Mitch...

He'd *kissed* her! And, to her everlasting shame and with no small amount of confusion, she'd kissed him back. *Kissed* him! He'd put something in her drink. He'd hypnotized her. He'd sold his soul to the devil in return for evil powers. Nothing on this earth could have compelled her to kiss Mitch Slater. Not of her own free will.

She stared again at her face in the mirror. Her cheeks were pink just remembering what had happened. How he'd held her tight around her waist so she was up against his hips. How he'd shifted that little bit so that she felt his...

No. It couldn't be real. How was it possible that Mitch Slater was a man? He was a journalist. Anyone who knew anything knew that a journalist couldn't be a man. Not a trustworthy man. Not a man to count on. Not a man to kiss back!

It had been her first lesson in college: Stay away from reporters! Don't get involved. They'll get the when and where from you, then leave the why as a memento to rehash in long nights of bitter contemplation. When she'd joined the *Times,* every woman between the age of eighteen and sixty had warned her about Mitch. He was dangerous. Sly. Smooth as twelve-year-old scotch. She'd seen his moves for herself, hadn't she? How he'd bend any rules, sneak behind enemy lines, bribe, cheat, connive for the sake of a story. Mostly *her* stories. So why in hell had she kissed him back?

Maybe it was the surprise. The shock. That had to be it. If she'd been herself it never would have happened. She'd never have lost her breath, never have felt the heat rise in her chest and never, never would have wanted more. It was a cruel joke from a trickster universe. Mitch Slater masquerading as her husband. Speaking to her parents. Calling her snookems.

He must be stopped.

She went to the sink and splashed cold water on her face. Immediately, she felt better, saner. She dug out some powder and her lipstick from her purse and applied them carefully. The world had not ended. No one had been hurt. It was simply a problem, and she'd handle it. Mitch was not going to spoil her life. Not now, not ever. The day Mitch Slater could outsmart her was the day she'd hang up her computer and get married for real.

She put her makeup away, brushed her hair, then

straightened her blouse. Once again, she was her old self, and that made her pulse ease and her thoughts grow logical.

First, she had to deal with Mitch. Get him off this island and away from her family. The longer he stayed, the greater the risk that he'd say something or do something that would expose the truth.

Second, she'd have to figure out what to do with him while he was here, even if that was just for an hour. He wanted to go up to the room? Great. At least there he wouldn't talk to anyone. Could she lock him in? There was that nice bellboy, Kimo. Maybe he could help her. Or maybe she could knock Mitch out cold with a really big, heavy, thick lead pipe and send him to the airport in the back of a taxi. She'd seen that done plenty of times on television. Only thing wrong with that plan was that she'd never met anyone with a harder head. He'd probably just get a concussion and sue her. But it might be worth it, just to hear the clunk.

She'd left him with Babs too long already. She'd figure out what to do once she was in the room with him.

Taking one last look at herself, she squared her shoulders and lifted her head. One step at a time. No need to panic. And no more kissing.

Despite her resolve, she found her step falter as she rounded the corner of the ladies' room. It was his laughter. Her mother's, too. It lifted into the air and caromed off the walls. Had she ever laughed that

way with Babs? She must have. Her childhood
hadn't been awful. She'd never been abused either
physically or mentally. She'd had everything she
ever wanted, and more. Dance classes, horseback rid-
ing lessons, piano tutors, perfect dresses. But for the
life of her, she couldn't remember that sound. Just
bright, carefree laughter. In school, yes. With Steph.
But with Babs? Laughter had been suspect then, cau-
tioned against. It was prideful somehow, arrogant. Or
common. Yes, common, not the other. Lesser people
laughed like that. Not the Brewsters.

Yet there was her mother, standing in front of
Mitch, holding her head back and letting go. It
wasn't a guffaw or anything half as gauche, but for
Babs it was a milestone.

What had Mitch said? What had tickled her mother
so much that she would react in such an abandoned
fashion? Was it something about her? Had Mitch told
her some revealing secret?

Bentley hurried now, even more anxious about
Mitch's ploy. He could do so much damage.

"Darling, your young man is a scamp! He's had
me laughing like I don't know what. Isn't that right,
Dan?"

Her father smiled, but it seemed to her he didn't
quite get the joke. He looked to Bentley, and for the
first time since she'd joined her family, she felt a
sense of connection. He gave her his look, his "Are
you all right, sweetie?" look. Just an eyebrow arch
and a slight dip of the chin. But she knew the mean-

ing, and more important, she understood the concern behind it. She nodded. Not enough for anyone else to notice. Just her dad.

"Ready to go up?"

Bentley turned to Mitch, and his broad smile took all the gentle sweetness she'd felt with her father and dashed it with cold water. The smug bastard. He had his hands folded across his chest as he leaned against one of the bar columns. His shirt, one of those awful retro things he always seemed to find, had a few wet spots on the front. Good. Maybe he'd throw it away. It was like something out of a fifties movie, something Dean Martin would have worn as he scored with some chicks. His slacks, somewhat more conservative, were more badly stained, particularly where she'd gotten him with that first glass of champagne. A normal man would have been embarrassed. He just looked terrifically pleased with himself, his plan, his whole miserable self. She'd see to it that didn't last long.

She looked into his brown eyes, certain she could awaken his shame with her glare. "All right, Carter," she said, keeping her voice low and tight. "Let's go up to the room."

It didn't work. Not her glare, not her tone, nothing. He just pushed himself off the bar and strolled toward her as if pretending to be someone's husband was as ordinary as using the telephone. As if he didn't know that he'd turned her life upside down.

"I've got my luggage by the front desk," he said,

that cocky grin of his making her wish she knew kickboxing.

"Swell."

"We'll see you at seven, Mom," Mitch said, stressing the term for Bentley's benefit. "I sure hope you hear from Stephanie. I'd hate for her to miss any of this."

Babs looked as though she wanted to talk about Stephanie for a while, but Bentley couldn't tolerate that. She grabbed Mitch by the arm and pulled him after her.

"She just can't get enough of me," Mitch said over his shoulder.

The grasp turned to a pinch.

"Ouch. You have to stop doing that."

"Then go home."

"No. I like it here."

When they were in the lobby and out of eye and earshot of her family, she swung on him, all the fury she'd been holding back right on the tip of her tongue. "You *like* it here? You *like* destroying my life? Can't you think of anything better to do with your twisted little mind? Like topple a government? Or—or reverse gravity?"

"I tried that last week. I couldn't figure out how to keep the change in my pockets."

"Oh man, you're asking for it."

"Yeah? This could get good."

Bentley looked around for a weapon. She spotted a heavy ashtray and lunged for it, but Mitch was too quick. He grabbed her around the waist and held her tight.

"Lemme go," she said, struggling against him. "I just want five minutes. That's all."

"Now, now. I'm pretty sure murder is illegal here, too."

"Not if I'm judged by a jury of my peers."

"Sexually repressed women?"

She turned, pushed at his chest, dug her heels into the carpet and pushed again. "Anyone with an IQ over ten!"

"Not bad. But you can do better."

She shoved at his arms, her hair flying into her face, but his grip kept her right up against him. Every time she moved, her breasts rubbed his chest, and that made her madder than anything. "Let… me…go."

He did. So fast she wheeled backward, her balance lost on the carpet. Back, back, until finally, the couch caught her legs and she sat. Hard.

She sprang up as fast as she could and pointed toward the door. "I want you off this island. Now."

"But it's a big island. Are you sure we can't share?"

"No. Go on. Get out."

"Uh…"

She turned toward the front desk. "Hello? Can someone help me, please? This man is very bad. He needs to be taken away."

"Very bad?" Mitch echoed.

She ignored him and concentrated on the hotel registration clerk. "You have to believe me. I'm telling the truth. I can show you letters. Give you phone numbers."

The woman behind the desk stared at her with growing alarm. "Are you all right, Miss?"

"No. I'm not. It's his fault." She pointed behind her at Mitch.

The clerk's gaze moved and her eyes widened. Bentley spun around and caught Mitch circling his ear with his index finger, the universal signal for nutcase. "Stop it," she told him, then looked back to the front desk. "It's not me. I swear."

"Darling, let's go on up, shall we? Dr. Redmond told us this might happen, remember?"

Bentley stopped. It was clear the poor clerk was confused. She actually believed him. It wasn't her fault, she supposed. Most women did believe him, at least in the beginning. It was his looks. Women wanted to believe in someone that pretty. Mitch knew it, too. He got away with murder for the same reason a dog licks his privates: because he could.

"Fine," she said with a sigh. "I give up."

Mitch took her hand in his and she didn't even bother to struggle. He led her through the lobby to the elevator. He pushed the Up button. "That was fun," he said.

"Shut up, Slater."

"No, really. I enjoyed it. You were really convincing."

The elevator opened, and he led her inside. Once the doors closed with their electronic whisper, he let her hand go. Bentley stared straight ahead, deciding right then that the best way to handle Mitch was to ignore him. Completely. Mitch who?

"So you want to start talking about Colker, sweetums?"

She read the menu posted on the side wall. Fresh mahimahi was the specialty of the house.

"You remember Colker? The reason you're here?"

But the sand dabs sounded good, too. With a nice salad on the side.

"I know you have information on him. Things will go a lot better if you just fess up."

Pineapple for dessert, of course. If she was feeling really sinful, she'd try the macadamia pie. But with the wedding cake, the dinners, the drinks, she'd probably have to forgo that pleasure.

The ding of her floor coincided with the slow stop of the elevator, and she entered the hallway looking neither right nor left. She felt something next to her, a gnat, a mosquito, but she ignored it.

"The silent treatment won't work, cookie. I've got you over a barrel."

She only slowed her pace a drop.

"One word to Mama and Carter's history, remember?"

Her shoulders sagged. She reached into her purse and pulled out the electronic card key and shoved it home. It had been a good few minutes, but he was right. He had her just where he wanted her. He could blow the whistle any second. And she didn't even have the information he was after. As far as she knew, Darren Colker was in Paraguay. But she doubted Mitch would believe her.

She entered the room. Mitch closed the door and locked it behind them. When she'd first checked in, the room had seemed wonderful. Large, bright, sunny. Luxurious, too. Now it felt like a prison.

"Look, Slater," she said, turning to him with as much earnestness as she could muster. "You're barking up the wrong tree. I'm here for my sister's wedding. Period. I'm not on a story, I don't know anything about Colker, and I'm not trying to get a scoop. I'm the matron of honor. That's all."

His smile was hesitant at first and her hope swelled. Then it became his patented, cocky grin and she knew he didn't believe her.

"You're good, Bentley," he said. "You almost had me there."

"I don't have the energy for this."

"For what? Trying to keep the story to yourself?"

She shook her head. "You. I don't have the energy for you. You're too much. You don't listen. You don't stop and think."

"Sure I do."

"No. You have it all figured out in your head and go blundering around, not really caring if you have it right or not."

His gaze shifted and intensified. He leaned a bit forward, and Bentley thought she'd finally caught his attention.

"I'm telling the truth," she said. "Can't you see that?"

"Well, let's take a look," he said. "We've known each other for over three years. Worked together, gone after the same stories, played a few games of poker on a late night. And all that time, you told me, you told everyone—including your own parents— that you were happily married to a CNN newscaster named Carter DeHaven. And now you say you're not here to investigate Darren Colker?"

"Right."

"I'm gonna be on you like white on rice, got it? I'm gonna tail you so close, you'll itch and I'll scratch. Because, honey, I don't believe one word you're saying."

Bentley heard him. She heard him good. He wouldn't listen to reason. He didn't believe the truth. There was only one thing left to do: outsmart Mitchell Slater and send him back to Los Angeles with his tail between his legs, so he'd never, under any circumstances, divulge her secret to a living soul.

Let the games begin.

Chapter Four

Bentley bit the inside of her cheek as hard as she could. She didn't let go until she felt tears well in both eyes. It was a technique she'd mastered in grammar school, one she had always been able to count on. She batted her lashes a few times, sniffed twice and made sure that she was close enough to Mitch that he could get the full effect of the crying whammy.

She sniffed once more, louder, and then she hit pay dirt. Mitch's smug grin faded. She turned just a bit to her left, so that the clouds outside would frame her face.

"What's this?" Mitch asked, the suspicion in his voice a little too clear.

"What?" she said, innocence itself.

"The crying game."

"I don't know what you mean." She moved to the window and stared at the ocean, her back as straight as she could make it. She fought the urge to giggle.

"Cut it out, Bentley. It won't work."

"Okay," she whispered. Meryl Streep had nothing on her.

"No. I mean it."

"I…" She let the word float alongside the dust motes. If she knew Mitch, which unfortunately she did, he'd go crazy with that one word. He was the kind of guy who couldn't leave if someone knocked "shave and a haircut" and didn't finish with "two bits." He liked closure, wrapping things up, seeing *The End* written out, not implied. So this, this lone pronoun, was doing its job. Making him wacko.

He walked behind her. She didn't turn. She could feel his frustration coming to a boil. Twenty more seconds. Ten.

"What already?" He grabbed her by the arm and spun her around. "I what?"

This was too easy. Like shooting fish in a barrel. "It's just that the consequences…"

He nodded, leaned toward her, tried to will her to finish her sentence. "The consequences…?"

"Carter wasn't just a convenience. He was… He was…" She looked away and made her lower lip tremble.

"What?" he said, loudly, impatiently.

"He was a gift. To my mother."

"A *what?*"

She sniffed. "A gift. A last request, you might say." She chanced a look at him, and she wasn't pleased with what she saw.

"So who's dying? You or Babs?"

"I don't know how you can be so cavalier."

"Easy. I don't believe you."

She turned to him sharply. "You don't think I would lie about something like this, do you?"

He nodded. "Sure."

"I..."

"You what? I know you're healthy. I go to the same doctor, remember?"

"You asked about me?"

"Well, sort of. Your file was just lying there."

"You read my medical file?"

He nodded.

"Why?"

"I'm a reporter."

"No, you're a snoop. That's got to be against the law. I could have you arrested."

He shook his head. "Sorry, babe. Try again."

She walked away from Mitch, furious beyond words. "I don't believe you."

"That's my line."

She whirled, facing him again. "I want you out of here. Now."

"But, snookems. Mom and Dad are expecting us for dinner."

"They are *not* your parents."

"They think they are."

"I'll tell them you had a story in Aruba. In Guatemala. In outer space."

"I'm not budging. Not until you tell me about Colker."

"I don't know anything about Colker. Dammit, what's it going to take to convince you?"

"The truth."

"I'm telling you the truth."

"Just like you told me about Carter?"

Bentley went to the couch and sat down. Suddenly she was tired. Tired of Mitch, of Carter. Of her whole family. "She wouldn't leave me alone," she said.

"Who?"

"Babs."

"Ah."

She stared at her shoes, not willing to watch his reaction. "She wants me married. Preferably pregnant. She never let up. Men were constantly showing up at my door. Unbelievable men. Horrible men. All with money, lots of it. And breeding. Can't forget that."

"So why didn't you tell her to stop?"

Now she looked at Mitch. The stain on his pants had dried, but she could still see the outline of the wet spot. That had been nice, hadn't it? One perfect moment in a day that would live in infamy. "Telling Babs to stop is like waving a red flag at a bull. It just makes her more determined."

"So Carter was your way of getting her to back off."

"Yes."

Mitch went to the honor bar and pulled out a beer.

He held it up for her, but she shook her head no. He closed the fridge and popped the top. "The odds of pulling off a scam like that are maybe one in a hundred. You should have stuck with something simple. Something that couldn't be proven."

"Like what?"

"Like, say, telling her you don't like boys."

"You think that would stop her from marrying me off?"

He took a long drink, then moved over to where she sat. He perched on the edge of the couch. "Okay, then how about telling her you couldn't have kids."

"Why would that have worked?"

"Because your mother wants a grandchild. More than anything."

"You've known her for fifteen minutes."

"And the subject of kids came up three times that I can remember."

"So?"

"So if you can't have them, she wouldn't care so much if you were married or not."

"Why is that better than Carter?"

"Because a person can be tracked down."

She shook her head. "If you hadn't stuck your nose into my business, it would have worked fine."

"It would have worked longer, but it would have blown up in the end."

"I'm sure you have a very interesting theory about that, Mitch, but I'm tired. I want to shower, and I want to take a nap."

"Okay."

She stood and walked to the door. Opening it wide, she pointed to the hall. "Take your bag with you."

Mitch shook his head. "Sorry, snookems. I'm here for the duration."

"You're really not going to leave."

He shook his head once more.

Bentley sighed. She shut the door and leaned her cheek against the cool wood for a second. "I'm not going to give up, you know. I'm going to figure out a way—"

"To kick me out. Right. But in the meantime, I'm going to get the story of a lifetime. I'm going to find Colker, and I'm going to get an interview. If you're very nice, I'll let you help me."

She laughed. His arrogance was an art form. "Why don't you go look for him now so I can get some rest?"

He stood up and put his beer on the end table. "I've got to change." He reached for his zipper.

"Hey!"

"What?"

"I don't want to know you that well."

"Spoilsport."

She went to the closet and grabbed her robe. "I'll be out soon. Don't touch anything." Then she made her escape into the bathroom—the only place she could be alone to think.

Mitch stared at the closed door. He thought about

Bentley, behind that door, taking off her clothes. It was inappropriate, sure, but it was also fun. He had few out-and-out immediate goals. One was to get the scoop on Colker. The other, which he hadn't realized he'd wanted until about twenty minutes ago, was to know Bentley Brewster in the biblical sense. It was a dangerous mission, fraught with peril. But he had the very strong sense that it would be worth it.

She was a liar. A cheat. A spoiled rich girl. And he wanted her more than a Pulitzer.

In the meantime, he needed to get his first priority taken care of. Colker was here. Despite the lady's protestations, the man was in residence. Mitch felt it in his gut. He'd learned to trust his instincts over the years. Yep, Colker was here. Now all he had to do was figure out how to get to him.

It wasn't as if he *planned* to go through her luggage. Hell, he did have a few scruples. But could he help it if Bentley had been careless? That she'd left her big suitcase unlocked? That if he knocked into the luggage stand a couple of times, the damn thing would fall and flap open?

He picked up the Louis Vuitton case—it must have cost a week's salary—and put it back on the stand. First he looked in the side pockets. Shoes, hair spray, belts, makeup, more hair stuff. In other words, nothing. Standing very still, he listened for a moment; the reassuring sound of the running water made him smile. Then he started looking through the clothes. Which was fine and dandy until he got to the Victoria's Secret portion.

The number on top was red. Silky and red. Silky and red and tiny. He lifted it with one finger. It was a teddy, probably the skimpiest damn teddy ever made. He could see right through it. His cheeks felt warm, and he wondered when Bentley had turned up the heat in the room. It wasn't hard to picture her wearing the tiny garment. Not hard at all. However...

He dropped the red item and picked up the white one. This was a bra, it seemed. A strapless bra with half-moon cups. Cups that would hold her breasts softly yet firmly. Had she turned the heat all the way up?

He let the bra go and went to the wall thermostat. It read seventy degrees. Time to call maintenance. After turning it down all the way, Mitch went back to the suitcase. What would he find next? A G-string? Tassels? He lifted the strapless bra once more and put it aside, his gaze transfixed by the scrap of material that had been exposed. It was tiny. Smaller even than the teddy. It was also pink. The kind of pink that made him think of champagne and strawberries. Of breathy voices and slow teasing. It was a pair of panties. Bentley's panties. Holy...

Was this the kind of thing she always wore? Hurrying now, afraid she'd come out of the shower any second, he riffled through the rest of her underwear. Every single piece was a ten on the sexy meter. Every one. Hadn't she ever heard of cotton?

He shoved everything back in and closed the suitcase, his face still warm and his pulse revved. So every day for the past two years, Bentley Brewster-DeHaven had worn *that* under her clothes. Under her nice, neat, tidy, conservative pantsuits, and her long-sleeved sweaters, and her dresses with the buttons up to here, she'd been wearing *little itty-bitty panties.* Worse. She'd been wearing *teddies.*

The nerve. The gall. She was a total fraud. Well, what could he expect from a woman who invented a goddamn husband? Who knew all about Colker and refused to tell him one bloody thing.

Colker. He hadn't found her notes. He listened again, but somewhere along the way the winds had picked up, strong enough even here on the fourteenth floor to mask the sound of the shower. Surely Bentley would come out now.

Damn it, he hadn't changed clothes. He raced to his bag, *not* Louis Vuitton or any Frenchman for that matter, and tugged on the zipper. The hanging bag flopped open, spilling his shaving kit and his plain, white, sensible boxer shorts onto the ground. Quickly gathering his things, he shoved them in a dresser drawer, then turned back to his bag. Dinner. Right. Something nice. Not jeans, not Dockers. Dress pants.

In a second, he had them off the hanger and had his current pants down and off. He kicked them away, then struggled with the buttons of his shirt. Finally, that was off, too. Just as he went for the new pants he heard the bathroom door open.

"I see looking through my luggage took longer than you'd planned."

He turned. Bentley stood by the luggage rack. Her arms were folded across her chest, her hair hidden inside a tall swirl of towel. The robe she wore was thick terry cloth, white. Nothing like the rest of her underwear. Her face, clean and scrubbed free of makeup, was remarkably beautiful in the lamplight. When had the room become so dark? When had Bentley become a woman?

"Well?"

"I don't know what you're talking about."

"Oh, please. You and I both know that you rifled through my things. You wouldn't be Mitch if you didn't."

"So why did you leave it unlocked?"

She walked toward him. He watched her gaze travel quickly over his almost naked body, resting a little too long on his boxers. Heat rushed through him again, but this time it went south instead of north. He felt some movement, some interest, some pressure. He spun around and reached for his pants.

"I left it unlocked so you would go through my things. So you would see I didn't have any information about Colker. That I didn't bring my computer. I didn't even bring a notebook. I'm here for the damn wedding and that's all!"

It was no use. He had to excuse himself. The shower was probably out of hot water, which was a good thing. A necessary thing. Where was his shirt?

"Hello? Did you hear anything I just said?"

There it was. It wasn't a designer shirt or anything, but it would do. Then he went to the dresser and pulled out his shaving kit and a pair of drawers.

"Am I not speaking words? In English?"

He took a few steps toward the bathroom, then backed up until he could reach for his beer. He had to reshuffle his handful, but it was worth it. Nothing went with a cold shower like a lukewarm brewski.

"Mitch Slater, you stop right there. Don't you dare ignore me." A thunderclap emphasized her statement, but he really, really couldn't stop to chat right now.

"We'll argue when I get out," he said, and then the door was closed behind him.

He sagged against the door and let the bundle in his arms fall to the floor. All except the beer. Taking a swig, he went into the shower and turned on the cold water. He shouted, loud, when he stepped inside, then shouted again for good measure. It was freezing. But it did the trick.

It took him about three minutes to realize he hadn't taken off his shorts.

Chapter Five

Bentley was sure Hawaii had excellent mental health professionals. Perhaps the hotel could recommend someone. Someplace. Preferably with bars on the windows and lots of padded rooms. Mitch was clearly off the beam. One taco short of a combo platter. And he planned on staying with her, in her room. Well, Mitch Slater hadn't seen the true power of Bentley Brewster. But he soon would.

She whipped the towel from her head and went through her rifled suitcase until she found her brush. While she combed, she picked out a suit for tonight's dinner, then dressed as hurriedly as possible, certain Mitch was going to exit the bathroom the moment she was naked. Somehow, she managed to get fully clothed without having to deal with shower boy.

Makeup would wait. So would her hair. What had to be done now was to deal with the Mitch problem.

She went to the phone, and as she sat, a brilliant stroke of lightning lit up the sky. Her gaze went to the window. The storm that had merely threatened this morning was in full glory now. The rain hit the glass hard and the wind played with the droplets like a swirl-a-paint. The clouds, which she could only see when lightning illuminated the sky, were thick and as black as coal. She'd never been in a hurricane before. Earthquakes, yes. Even a tornado once. But never a hurricane.

Maybe she could tell Mitch to go collect some seashells. Then the water surge could carry him away, and she'd have her life back.

She smiled at the thought as she reached for the phone. Before she could grab the receiver, it rang, scaring her enough to make her jump. It rang once more, the red light next to it blinking with urgency.

She lifted the receiver. "Hello?"

"The hurricane isn't supposed to be this close. I was told that there would be no problems on this island. Stephanie can't get a plane to bring her here, and I've spent over fifty thousand dollars on her wedding. I can't find Jack, Aunt Tildy wants to go home, it's very possible the hotel will lose electricity and what the hell am I supposed to do with ten thousand dollars' worth of wilted orchids? I swear, I can't handle this, Bentley. I just can't."

"Hi, Mother."

"Hmm?"

"I said... Never mind. Are you and Daddy dressed for dinner?"

"Of course."

"Then we'll talk about all of this in a half hour, okay? I have some business to take care of."

"What possible business could you have that's more important than your sister's wedding? I think this selfishness is very unattractive, dear. I'll wager Carter does, too."

Bentley felt the button being pushed, right in her solar plexus. It was an old button, born many years ago, developed slowly and carefully every time Bentley had a thought that was contrary to her mother's. She'd been selfish all her life, and Babs took great joy in pointing this out to her on every possible occasion.

"Mother, I can't do anything about the hurricane. I'm not a meteorologist. I can't fly Stephanie here myself. I'm not a pilot."

"I don't care for that sarcasm."

Bentley took a deep breath. "I'm sorry, Mother. I know you're under a lot of stress. But we'll be at dinner in a few minutes. I promise I'll be as sympathetic as Father Flanagan."

There was a considerable pause, and Bentley felt sure Mitch would come out any second. How much did he have to wash, for goodness' sake?

"It's not easy, you know," Babs said in her patented martyr's voice. "You girls have always been the most important thing."

"I know that, Mom. Come on. Put on your Harry Winston diamonds. Those always make you feel better."

"Daddy made the reservations under his name."

Bentley rolled her eyes. Never once in the history of her family life had reservations been made under any other name. "Okay," she said, trying to sound chipper.

"And try and do something about your hair, dear. This morning's look didn't suit you."

She was about to mention that she'd been on a five-hour plane ride this morning, but what was the use? "I'll try. See you soon." She hung up before Babs could poke her again.

She lifted the cradle once more, but she didn't dial. The storm captured her attention once more and a sudden gust of ennui swirled around her, settling on her shoulders. Why did she give her mother the power to do this to her? In every other aspect of her life she was an adult. Fully capable of getting stories on Mafia hit men, drug kingpins, government officials. But when Babs spoke, she became a child again.

It was her own fault. Babs was Babs and would be Babs forever. Nothing was going to transform her into a Disney mom. The only thing that could be changed was how she let Babs affect her.

The door to the bathroom opened. Mitch, his hair wet, barefoot and dressed in black slacks and a white shirt, stood silhouetted in light. From this angle, his features were blurry, indistinct. But her breath caught in her throat. Because everything about the man in the light was exactly, to the inch, Carter. All she imagined her husband would be.

Tall, almost up to the top of the door frame. Wide in the shoulders and slim in the hips. Straight, with an arrogance that came from experience, not wishful thinking. And exuding sex like a perfume sample at the Estée Lauder counter.

"You're dressed," he said.

"What were you expecting?"

"You're dressed but your hair isn't done."

She turned her head a bit to the side. "Hello? You were in the bathroom. Where was I supposed to do my hair? In the closet?"

He strode into the main room, his face coming into focus, and her fanciful thoughts shattered like broken glass. He might have the body of Carter, but his personality? Not even close. Miles apart. Light years apart.

"So, get cookin'. Mom and Dad are expecting us in fifteen minutes."

"It drives me insane when you call them that."

Mitch grabbed a pair of socks from his bag, then sat on the bed to put them on. She didn't like him on the bed. Even when he had all his clothes on.

"I think Carter would call them Mom and Dad."

"You're not Carter."

"Carter doesn't exist."

"So how do you know what he'd call my parents?"

He stared at her for a long beat, his right eyebrow

cocked and his lips pressed together. "This conversation isn't very productive. Why don't you go put your hair up, huh? I've got to make a call."

"To whom?"

He got up and walked toward her. He seemed far too tall and daunting from her perch on the couch.

"I'm calling the restaurant, if that's any of your business."

She hugged the receiver closer to her chest. "Why?"

He leaned down. She could see his cheeks were smooth and clean shaven, smell his soft hint of spicy cologne, measure the width of his shoulders against the wall behind him.

"Because I want to order some wine. Ahead of time. Is that okay with you?"

She gave him another look, this time focusing on his face, not his physique. "I don't trust you."

"Good girl."

"Don't call me that."

"Good woman."

"I don't like you at all, you know."

He nodded. "Can I have the phone anyway?"

She looked at the receiver in her hand, then slowly held it out to Mitch. When he took it, his fingers brushed against hers, and the sky lit up like the Fourth of July. She jerked back, grateful to realize that it was just lightning. Not her own reaction. Then she looked up and saw that Mitch was looking at her as if she'd changed from a pumpkin to a coach.

"Lightning," she said.

He nodded. But she doubted somehow he'd heard her. His gaze was on her face, unwavering, intense. He was seeing something new, she could tell by the way his brows arched. But what? What did he see when he looked at her that way? That hungry way?

"It was a jolt all right," he said, his voice husky.

She got up. Walked quickly to her bag. Grabbed her hair blower and her brush. "So, I thought you were going to make a phone call?"

"And I thought I was immune."

She spun toward him. "What?"

"Immune. You've always just been the competition."

"And?"

"And now you're more."

She nearly said something smart-ass. But another bolt of lightning lit up the room just then, and when she saw his face, it was like seeing *him* for the first time. There was no smart-ass comment to make. Because she knew exactly what he meant.

THE ELEVATOR WAS CROWDED, this being the dinner hour. Everyone was talking about the weather. A short man with bad breath next to Bentley announced that the only road to or from the hotel had a history of washing out. His companion, an older woman with bottle-red hair mentioned that on the news they were calling this hurricane Bonnie, and that this island was only getting the outskirts of the impact. The short man asked if this was the outskirts, what kind of nightmare would the inskirts be?

Bentley smiled at Mitch's grin. Then they reached the lobby, and the door whispered open. Voices, lots of them, surprised her. It had been so quiet when she'd arrived. They turned the corner to the main lobby and she saw who the voices were connected to: every guest in the hotel. The lobby was jammed. People dressed in bathing suits and women dressed in sequined gowns all hummed around the central desk like bees in a hive. Tension flew hot and heavy, and that was only partially a result of the winds shrieking outside the doors. These were mostly honeymoon couples from the Midwest, or the Bible Belt. They didn't know a hurricane from a volcano, and they were scared.

Mitch took her arm and led her through the crowd. She kept hearing the word "flashlight," and she remembered that she had one—she always took a flashlight with her when she traveled. It was in her suitcase. But did it work? "We have to get batteries," she said, tugging Mitch to slow down. "I've got a flashlight, but I think I need new batteries."

"You've got a flashlight?"

She nodded. "I always keep emergency supplies on hand. Flashlight, some waterproof matches, a thermal blanket, food bars, first aid kit. You know."

He shook his head. "And I thought your desk was bad."

"You'll be happy to use my supplies, no doubt."

"Well, yeah."

"There's only enough for one."

He turned to her, finally coming to a stop. "Now, you shouldn't lie to me, Bentley. You and I both know that deep in your heart you're a little Mother Teresa. You've brought enough supplies for half the people here, am I right?"

"No." He cocked his eyebrow. The one she wanted to rip off with her bare hands. "So what if I bring extras?" she said. "I'm just a nice person, that's all."

"You're all the things a newsman shouldn't be, kiddo. And nice is number one on the list."

That one got her. She pulled her arm free of his, her anger as wild as the night outside. "You watch yourself, Slater. I've beat you out of too many stories for you to start with that."

"Now, now, don't get all upset."

"Why not? You've basically told me I'm no good at my job."

"I didn't mean it that way."

"No? What way did you mean it?"

He finally clued in that she was really steamed. She could see it in his expression, the surprise in his eyes. And the fact that he took two steps back.

"Hey," he said, his voice much softer and not all full of his normal sarcasm. "I'm sorry. Really. I was just shooting off my mouth. You're a good journalist, Bentley. That's why I hate you so much. If you weren't a threat, we'd have slept together months ago.''

She would *not* smile. ''You're wrong again, kiddo. We wouldn't have slept together. Ever. I don't go for your type.''

He grinned at her, flashing the charm that had won a hundred ladies. ''What type is that?''

''Unprepared.''

He shook his head, his smile still too arrogant to be legal, then tapped his back pocket. ''Wrong again, sunshine. I'm always prepared for what really counts.''

''Oh, I forgot. You've always got your brains where you need them.''

''Touché. Or should I say tushie.''

''Your sophistication is no match for me. I'm going to the shop over there to get my batteries. Why don't you go outside and fly a kite.''

''I love it when you talk like that, snookems. It makes me hot all over.''

''Oh, get over yourself.'' She turned abruptly, elbowing a man in a gaudy Hawaiian shirt. Her apology was brief, then she was making her way through the crowd. She felt more than saw Mitch on her heels.

Their conversation had been foolish, childish even. Yet somehow she felt exhilarated. He'd made her think. He kept her on her toes. Dammit.

The line at the little gift shop was long. Everyone was getting supplies, and the poor girl behind the counter seemed quite overwhelmed. Waiting might make them late for dinner, and Babs would have a stroke.

She turned to Mitch and caught him eyeing a leggy brunette in a butt-floss bikini. "Oh my God," she said, grabbing his arm. "I don't believe it."

"What?"

"Colker!"

That got his attention. The skinny brunette might as well have been a mango.

"Where?"

She searched the crowd, giving Mitch a chance to see her intense expression from three different angles. Finally, she pointed toward the elevators. "There."

"Where?" Mitch got up on his toes to look, craning to see between the crowds, the foliage, the pillars.

"I really think that's him. You stay here. I'll go find out. Get double-A batteries. As many as you can." She set off, but before she'd taken two steps, he caught the back of her suit jacket and pulled her back.

"Hold it."

"Let go. I'm losing him."

"I don't believe you."

"Then let go."

"What did he look like?"

"You know what he looks like. Short, bald on top, long white hair in the back. Glasses. Bad chin."

"And you really saw him?"

"I'd like to find out."

"I'll go."

"Not a chance!"

"You have to get your supplies. And see your parents."

"Oh, so suddenly they're *my* parents."

"Unless you want them to find out I'm not their son, yeah."

She gave him her most vicious glare. "That's not fair."

"You're right." He walked quickly toward her, grabbed her around the waist and pulled her to him. He kissed her, once, hard, then let her go. "If I'm not back by tomorrow, send a hula dancer." With that, he was off. Pushing his way through the crowd, getting several angry gestures for his trouble.

Bentley smiled. Sighed. Mentally patted herself on the back. That would teach him.

MITCH SAW HIM. At least he thought that was him. The guy was bald on top, but his white hair wasn't all shaggy and long in the back. But Colker had access to barbers. The man had gone into the men's room. Good thing he wasn't chasing a woman.

Moving quickly and trying not to step on anyone else's toes, Mitch made his way into the bathroom. It was big, plush and crowded. He scanned the faces in his immediate vicinity, but no Colker. Then he ventured toward the stalls. It wasn't polite to stare in there, especially at the men in the stalls, so he had to do things slowly, carefully. One by one, he eliminated the contenders. Until he got to stall number six.

It could be Colker. He had the right build, and except for the length of his hair, he was a perfect match. Without taking his eyes off the man, Mitch went to the sink and washed his hands. He could see number six in the mirror now, and it was clear Colker was finished.

He turned. Mitch turned. It wasn't Colker.

Had he lost him? Or was this the man Bentley had seen?

Or, which suddenly seemed most likely, had Bentley just sent him on a wild-goose chase? What the hell was wrong with him? He should have seen her scheme from the get-go. That woman had done something to his logic. She'd bamboozled him, right there in the lobby.

It was going to be fun to pay her back.

"I REALLY DON'T SEE WHY we can't go to the other restaurant."

"Because we're here already, Bentley. This is where we made our reservations."

"We can make new reservations, Mother."

"Not if we want to eat anytime before midnight. Look at the crowd here."

Bentley did. The place was packed, even though it was the most expensive restaurant on the island. Guess everyone wanted a wonderful last meal. But it screwed up her grand plan, and that wasn't good. Mitch would find them here. Right after he figured out that she hadn't seen Colker at all. He'd be upset, too. What a shame.

"So sit down and look at the menu," Babs said. "Where did you say Carter was? Is he going to be here in time for dinner?"

"I hope not."

"What?"

Bentley looked up. "I hope he will be. The line at the store was pretty long."

"Why do you need batteries, dear? I heard on the TV that this island isn't going to be hit too hard. Surely the electricity won't go out."

"Just in case, Mother."

"Well, just in case isn't going to get Stephanie here."

Bentley would have worried over the non sequitur if someone else had said it. For her mother, the logic was there, just private.

She looked at the menu. It was damn pricey here. Even the pasta was over twenty bucks. Just Babs's style. Why eat if you couldn't overpay?

"May I get you a drink, ma'am?"

Bentley looked up at the waiter. He was the guy who carried her luggage in. Kimo. Or was he? She looked for a name tag but couldn't find one. "Scotch. A double. On the rocks."

"Bentley!"

"What?" She turned to her mother, feeling exasperated as always. "What?"

"Don't you think you've had enough hard liquor today? Daddy and I are getting champagne."

"You can get just as drunk on champagne, Mother. It just takes longer and leaves you with a headache."

"I don't like this scotch business."

"That's why I didn't order any for you."

"Bentley!"

She smiled at her mother, then turned again to the waiter. "Make it a triple," she said, but quietly, just so he could hear. He nodded.

"I'm thinking about getting the mahimahi," her father said, blithely unconcerned with the mini battle that had just taken place. "It looks good."

"Get it broiled, Danny. You know you have to watch your heart."

"I'm on vacation, Babs. I can have butter on vacation."

"You think your arteries know we're in Hawaii?"

"The hell with my arteries."

"Bentley, say something to him."

"I'll drink to that, Pop."

Babs slammed her menu down on the table. Her Harry Winston diamond necklace glittered in the candlelight. Bentley was amazed, as always, at her mother's beauty. She was a remarkably striking woman for her age, or any age. If only she weren't insane.

"I don't think either of you are very nice. You know the stress I'm under, and all this bickering isn't doing me one bit of good."

First she was too nice, now not nice enough. Boy, this was a tough crowd. "Sorry, Mom. I really am. Have you heard from Stephanie?"

Babs sat back in the big booth and sighed dramatically. She should have a spotlight on her for the upcoming performance.

"There were no outside lines available from the hotel," she said. "Not one. This is supposed to be a four-star hotel. I'm going to find out who runs this place and give them a piece of my mind."

"They're not responsible for natural disasters, Mother."

"They have a responsibility to their guests. I chose this place because the wedding coordinator told me it would be perfect. That I wouldn't have to worry about a thing. All I'd have to do was show up. Now look. Everything's going wrong. And Stephanie. Poor Stephanie."

Bentley didn't want anyone to get hurt or anything, but where the hell was the storm surge when she needed it. A nice wall of water would be perfect right about now.

She glanced up as the waiter came back to the table, anxious for her scotch. But it wasn't the waiter. It was Mitch. Smiling, audacious, cocky.

"Well, that was fun, honey lamb," he said. Then he looked at her mother. "Mom, it's great to see you. We have so much to talk about."

Chapter Six

Mitch's satisfaction grew as he watched Bentley's expression change from surprise to alarm to panic. Good. She deserved all she was going to get. He'd teach her to play nice if it killed them both.

Mitch debated where to sit. Next to Babs would give him a good view of Bentley, and it would keep him a relatively safe distance from Bentley's pinches, too. On the other hand, there was no way Babs Brewster could smell half as good as her daughter.

He went to Bentley's side. "Scoot over."

She glared at him for a few seconds, then reluctantly moved toward her father, leaving Mitch barely enough room to sit down.

"Forgive me, Mom and Dad. The line at the gift shop was brutal. But I didn't want to disappoint my honey-bunch. She does need her batteries."

"She's not going to need them this time," Babs said. "There won't be any call for a flashlight."

"Flashlight?" Mitch said, widening his eyes with

surprise. Then he turned to his darling wife. "You didn't tell me you brought a flashlight."

"Why else would she need batteries?" Babs asked.

Bentley got hold of his thigh just as he opened his mouth. She pinched him as hard as she could, but he forced himself not to react. "It's kind of private," Mitch whispered, loud enough for Babs, Danny and the couple behind them to hear. "Intimate, if you know what I mean."

Babs looked at him crookedly for a moment, then her cheeks became infused with pink. "Oh, heavens."

"That's my Bentley," Mitch announced proudly.

'His' Bentley looked ready to kill him. "He's joking, Mother."

"I see."

Mitch gave Babs a broad wink. It worked, too. Babs picked up her menu and hid behind it. Bentley took the opportunity to turn on Mitch and mouth her displeasure. He was able to make out each one of the words as most of them contained only four letters.

He smiled at her. His work here was not done, though. Not nearly done.

"I'll get you for this," she whispered, just loud enough for him to hear.

He broadened his smile. "There's actually a real cute story about her, um, equipment. Honey, you want to tell them? Or should I tell them about the other thing?''

The panic in her eyes nearly made him laugh out loud. It was clear she thought he was about to tell her mother and father a completely undignified lie about her or spill the beans about Carter. Oh, she of little faith. Well, maybe this would teach her not to mess with Mitch Slater.

''I don't think that was my story, Carter,'' Bentley said, the pleading evident in her voice. ''It must have been someone you knew before we met.''

''No, no. I'm surprised you don't remember.'' He leaned over to grab her cheek. ''Or is my snookems just shy?''

She batted his hand away, then smiled at her mother. The color in Bentley's cheeks was almost the exact shade as her mother's blush.

He was just about to change the subject and ease Bentley's mind when the waiter appeared. He handed Bentley her drink, scotch from the looks of it, and served the rest of them champagne.

While Babs ordered hors d'oeuvres, Bentley leaned very close to him, placing her mouth right next to his ear. ''You watch yourself, Carter,'' she whispered fiercely. ''I'm warning you.''

''Or what?''

''Or I'll have to do something drastic.''

''I'd like to see you try.''

''Don't. I'm not kidding.''

"I'm not, either. Maybe next time when you spot Colker, it'll really be Colker."

"To this horrible hurricane's disappearance," Babs announced, holding up her flute.

"Here, here," Mitch said, feeling so good now, the champagne might be a downer.

"I want the mahimahi," Danny said.

Babs gave Dan a smoldering look, and Mitch realized that's where Bentley got the gene. They were good at it, these Brewster women.

"Hey, did I ever tell you folks about our honeymoon?"

"No!" Bentley said. This time he caught her hand before she could deliver the pinch.

"Why, no," Babs said, smiling at him sweetly. "We'd love to hear about it."

"Well, it's a cute story."

Bentley started coughing.

"It all started with this little misunderstanding, see."

The coughing got louder. He also noticed that her scotch was coming near the edge of the table, toward his lap, and although he'd needed a cold shower earlier, he didn't need a repeat. He reached over with his right hand and took her glass, then with his left patted her on the back.

She gave him a look that would have killed most mortals, but he just kept patting away, looking as concerned as he knew how. "You okay, honey?"

Bentley turned quickly and grabbed his wrist before he could whack her again. "I'm fine. Thank you."

"Then can I continue?"

"Only if you don't value your life."

He laughed, then turned to Babs and Dan. "I could just eat her up with a spoon."

"Are you really all right, Bentley?"

"Yes, Mother. I'm peachy."

"Good, then let's hear your story, Carter. We so regretted not being there for your wedding. I still can't believe you two didn't even take one picture."

Bentley squeezed his wrist tighter. At least she didn't have liquid in her hand. A little squeezing he could stand.

"Oh, let's not talk about the honeymoon. It's boring. Honest."

"Bentley, you're too modest," he said. "So we were on our honeymoon, see, and Bent was so darn adorable. She didn't want to leave the room, and it had been five days—"

"*Honey,*" she said, breaking in quite deliberately. "Why don't you tell them about the time you got arrested for soliciting? It's a real scream, Mother. You'll love it."

He was on to her in a flash. "No, I'll tell them about that hilarious mix-up where you ended up stark naked on the steps of the *Times* building."

"That's not half as amusing as the time the governor found you in bed with his wife."

"What about that stunt you pulled with the jockey and the basketball player?"

"We can't forget about that piece in the *Enquirer.* You and Bubbles the chimp?"

"How about that time you sent your underwear to Walter Cronkite?"

"Children!"

Mitch looked at Babs, then back at Bentley. He'd won. At least, he thought he'd won.

"Perhaps we should settle down, hmm?" Babs said, as if talking to toddlers. "We're all hungry and tired. Ah, here's the waiter with the hors d'oeuvres. Carter, would you like to serve the crab cakes while I order Danny's mahimahi?"

Mitch smiled, but he wasn't happy. Bentley was looking too pleased with herself. "Sure thing, Mom."

Babs handed her plate to him, and he used the fancy silver tongs to capture a little fried cake. He waited until they'd all ordered dinner before he passed her plate back. When he did, he winked at her and whispered, "I'll tell you about our honeymoon later. When Bentley isn't there to spoil the story."

Of course, Bentley heard him. He knew that because she pinched him again. In a very personal and highly sensitive area, just as he was scooping up another crab cake. He jumped, and the hors d'oeuvre flew straight up in the air and landed unceremoniously on Danny's plate. Dan began to eat immediately, not concerned in the least about the morsel's surprise flight.

Babs had caught the action, though, and she turned on Bentley. "What is the matter with you?" she said in a stage whisper that could have been heard in the second balcony. "Are you purposely trying to ruin this wedding?"

Mitch put his arm around Bentley. "It's my fault, Mother. I know Bentley's been on edge, and I haven't been very nice to her."

"That's kind of you, Carter, but if there's one thing my girls know how to do, it's behave. At least they used to."

"I'm sorry," Bentley said, removing his arm from her shoulder. "I don't know what came over me."

"It might be hormonal, dear," Babs said. "I'll give you the number of my psychiatrist."

When Mitch looked at her, she shrugged. "He prescribes."

Bentley just sighed. "Carter," she said, her words chock-full of emotion. "Could you please go to the gift shop and get me some aspirin? I've got a vicious headache."

"Maybe the waiter can find us some."

"*Carter.*" The emotion was still there, only now it was out-and-out anger. "Be a dear and get me some aspirin. You wouldn't want me to get all upset again, would you?"

"No. No. Be happy to oblige, honey-bunch." He

stood up, took a swig from his champagne, then bent close to her so he could whisper. "But I'll be back."

Bentley went for her scotch. Mitch left. Quickly.

When he was finally out of the restaurant, Bentley relaxed. She reached for her compact and did a quick emergency repair on her face, then turned to face her parents. The smile she pasted on was an old standby. She called it her Mona Lisa, not too broad, not too tight. Just right. What she really wanted to do was drink her scotch and chase it with a tequila shooter, but instead, she just tucked her napkin on her lap like a good girl. At least he hadn't won this round, she thought. As if he thought he could win. Not on this voyage, sailor.

"Bentley, I want you to tell me what's going on."

"Nothing. Really."

Her mother's look told her she'd have to do better.

"It's personal, Mother. Between Carter and me."

"You have to know he loves you, dear."

That stopped her. She took a sip of scotch. "Excuse me?"

Babs leaned forward so she could talk sotto voce. "I can see you two are having some trouble. I'm not blind. But it's very clear—" they were back to spoken words again "—that he loves you very much."

"How can you tell?"

"The way he looks at you, darling. Any fool can see he loves you beyond reason. I'd hoped he'd be a good man, Bentley. But even I never dreamed he'd be so perfect."

"You've known him for twenty minutes."

Babs shook her head. Bentley glanced at her father, but he was transfixed by the nearby dessert cart.

"I've known Carter since you were sixteen. When you used to tell me about your dream man. He was in your diaries. Remember? All of them."

"You read my diaries?"

"Carter is the one you've wanted your whole life, and you know it. I could have picked him out of a hundred men, a thousand."

"I don't have a response to that," she said. And it was true. She felt speechless and helpless because her mother's words were true. It hadn't been a fluke, that déjà vu feeling she'd had when Mitch had come out of the bathroom. It had been a memory, a piece of her past, a remnant of her childhood come to life. But Mitch?

"Bentley? Your color doesn't look good."

"I don't feel well, Mom. As a matter of fact, I feel awful." She grabbed her purse and scooted out of the booth. "Please tell Carter I've gone upstairs. Have him bring the aspirin, won't you?"

"Darling?"

She went near her mother and took her outstretched hand. "Hmm?"

"Try hard. Very hard. I think he's worth it."

She nodded, feeling the pressure of real tears behind her eyes. Blinking them away, she smiled, squeezed her mother's hand and left the dining room.

"Hey, you okay?"

Bentley came out of her snooze with a start. The room was dark, the wind still pushed at the windows, and she was in bed. Carter...Mitch was sitting next to her and his cool palm was resting gently on her forehead.

"What time is it?"

"Twelve-thirty."

She moved, and his hand disappeared, and for a crazy moment she wanted to reach out, grab it and pull it back. "I must have fallen asleep."

"You forgot your pj's," he said.

She lifted the comforter to peek underneath and saw she was still in the white suit, still in her panty hose. She had kicked her shoes off, at least.

"I brought you your aspirin. If that's what you really want."

She nodded. "Yeah. I do. Thanks."

He got up, and she didn't see him until he switched on the bathroom light. The room looked big with its shadows and sounded eerie with the howling wind just outside. Looking at Mitch's silhouette only made things worse. She hadn't been able to stop thinking about what her mother said. Even in sleep, she'd mixed up Mitch and Carter and her girlhood infatuations until she didn't know which end was up.

She heard the water flow from the tap as she sat up, pulling a pillow behind her. When Mitch came back, he switched on the main light.

"Oh, no. Turn it off."

"Sure thing, vampira."

Despite his attempt at humor, he obeyed, and once more in the dark, with only the thin light from the bathroom to lead his way, he came to her bed.

He waited until he sat before handing her the water and aspirin. The awareness of his body next to hers, the dip in the mattress where he sat, the palm he lifted toward her was enough to stir all her nerve endings into a state of wariness. When she touched him, just to get the aspirin, she fully expected another bolt of lightning to split the sky, and when it didn't she felt unexpectedly saddened.

Maybe her mother had been right about her hormones. She hadn't had a checkup in more than a year. Was it possible to go through the change in one's twenties?

It was difficult to swallow with her throat all tight, but she got the pills down. She wondered if the analgesic would have any effect on her, especially this awful feeling that Mitch meant more to her than his traditional role as pain in the butt.

"That was pretty good back there," he said. "You can take care of yourself, I'll say that much for you."

She smiled. "Yeah, I thought it was okay. Sure got the job done."

It was his turn to smile, and she wished she hadn't said anything amusing. She seemed to be in the most trouble when he looked like that—like he was a nice, handsome, funny, affectionate guy. Not a world champion jerk. It was very confusing.

"You know, I wasn't going to snitch."

"No?"

He shook his head. "Nope."

"Promise me you won't? Ever?"

He frowned. "Sorry, cupcake. That's my ace in the hole."

"Damn you."

"But I will tell you something I probably shouldn't."

"What's that?"

"I found Colker. The *real* Colker."

She narrowed her eyes, her mistrust blocking everything else from her mind and body. "Oh?"

"Don't say it like that. *I'm* not the one who faked it this evening, remember?"

"So how do you know? Did you see him?"

"Not exactly."

"How, exactly?"

"I talked to one of the clerks."

"Uh-huh. And what was her name?"

"Shelli. She said that there's a mysterious—" He jerked back a bit and gave her a suspicious look. "How'd you know it was a her?"

She didn't grace him with an answer. Just a look. An "Oh, please, as if you'd ever spend time with a male if there was a female within a hundred miles" look.

"Oh. Well, anyway, Shelli told me that there's this guy up in the penthouse. Very mysterious. Very private. No one knows his real name, no one goes in there to clean except two people who've been sworn to secrecy. Lots of electronic equipment, based on the usage, lots of room service left outside the door.''

"So you figure…''

"I figure he's our man. This is a honeymoon hotel, cookie, or haven't you noticed? He's a loner, our friend in the penthouse. A loner who's loaded.''

"You astound me with your journalistic skills. Honest. So when are you going to see Shelli again?''

"Tomorrow.'' He started to rise, then stopped. "Hey!''

"I'm not such a bad journalist myself, bucko.''

"You're just plain mean.''

She shook her head. "Nah. Just honest.''

His expression changed. It was still dark, and she could only make out the broad strokes of his features, but still she could tell something shifted. "So, honest one, tell me about the deal with Babs and Dan?''

"The deal?''

"Yeah. Why'd you really come up with this nutball scheme?''

"I told you.''

He shook his head. "The journalist in me says that was the cover story. I'm looking for the juice. Off the record, of course.''

"No way.''

"Yes way.''

She thought of turning on the light. Letting him see she wasn't kidding around anymore. Then she realized he probably knew that. Mitch was many things, but dumb wasn't one of them. "It's not very exciting. Not even amusing."

"Spill."

She shifted a bit, and he did, too. He moved closer to her on the bed. Close enough to touch. His thigh met her thigh, and the collision brought on a little too much heat. "You've met Babs. I would think that would explain everything."

"I've also met you. And that's the part that doesn't add up. I know you can be a real tiger when you need to. So why are you such a pussycat with Mom?"

She sighed. "Don't you have parents?"

He was quiet for too long. "Not so's you'd notice."

"Hatched, were you?"

"Might as well have been. Never met the old man. From what I know about my mother, I might have been better off not knowing her, either. But this isn't my turn."

His revelation didn't surprise her somehow. As a matter of fact, it made a few things fall into place. His behavior at the office, for one. He'd often reminded her of the Artful Dodger, and now she knew why. He'd been on his own from the beginning. A scrapper, her father would have said.

"Come on. I don't have all night."

"There's no good answer to your question, Mitch. The woman drives me up a wall. She's more persistent than anyone I've ever met. More driven than a taxi. She just doesn't let up.''

''Can you say no? I know you can.''

She grimaced at his joke. ''That's the point, Sherlock. With her, I can't say no.''

He sat still for a long while. Long enough for her to remember about his thigh. The heat. About the fact that the couch was very small and the bed was very big.

''That surprises me, Bentley. Honest, it does. I'll deny I ever said this, but you're pretty damn remarkable. When you get hold of a story, you're like a bulldog. You never let up. Huh. Just like Mom, eh? Maybe you two clash because you're too much alike.''

''I'm *not* like her.''

''Hey, chill. It was a compliment. Babs is a beautiful woman. She's successful. She's confident. What's not to like?''

''You want something, don't you? You want something really, really big. That's what this is about, isn't it? Either that or you've been drinking a lot more heavily than I realized.''

''I want something, all right.''

Again, a shift. She doubted she would have noticed had the lights been on. She would have been looking too hard. She *felt* this change. One minute his conversation had been safe and easy, and now, with that one little sentence, all bets were off. The red flag was up, and she had better find shelter. Fast.

"You've found Colker. What more could you want?"

Then he was leaning. Bracing his arms on either side of her body. It wasn't just his thigh that touched her now, but his chest, his arms. The heat expanded.

He kissed her.

Not like this morning. Not even like this evening. This time, he kissed her like he wanted to.

His lips were soft, warm. The pressure built slowly, stealing her senses. Then he opened his mouth just a little and teased her with his tongue. The winds screamed outside, the windows pulsed with the force.

Her lips parted of their own accord. He moved again, closer, tighter. He explored her more boldly, and she responded with a body that wasn't hers, wasn't wise. This was foolish. She couldn't be kissing Carter. Mitch. Him.

Something banged into the window, scaring the bejeezus out of both of them. Mitch moved back. She turned to the window. Whatever it had been was gone. Probably a palm frond or a tree limb.

Or her guardian angel.

When he turned back, she scooted away, breaking whatever spell he'd cast. "No, no, no. I don't think so."

He reached out and caught her wrist. "Think? Who said anything about thinking?"

"I'm not going to do this. Not with you."

"Why not? It was starting to be pretty terrific."

She jerked her wrist free, pushed back the covers and got out of bed. It was still cold in the room. When she'd come up from dinner, the place had been an icebox. Now it was just freezing. She moved to the door and flipped on the light. It took a moment for her eyes to adjust, and when they did she saw that Mitch, *Mitch Slater,* her sworn enemy and evil-doer, was the man she'd just kissed. Again.

"You are so slick," she said. "You know every trick in the book, don't you? You weasel your way into my private life, steal my husband's identity, take sides with my mother, go after my story, and now you want to hop into my bed, too?"

Mitch sprang from the bed. "Aha!"

"Aha?"

"Your story! *Your* story. I knew it. You call me slick. Ha! You're good, Brewster. Damn good. But not good enough."

"Oh, for God's sake. I didn't mean—"

"Of course you didn't mean it. You wanted to keep the lie going. You wanted Colker all to yourself. And I shared with you. Naughty, naughty Bentley. I should tell your mother on you."

"Certifiable. That's what you are. And, Mr. Genius Who Knows Every Damn Thing, where are you sleeping tonight?"

He pointed to the bed. "Right here, Mrs. De-Haven."

"Not in this lifetime."

"Don't flatter yourself. I want to sleep. Period."

"Right. And that kiss was just between colleagues. I suppose you'd kiss Carl Bernstein the same way?"

"Carl's married. For real."

She stomped to the bed and pulled one pillow off, then tossed it onto the couch. "That's where you're going to sleep, buddy, and if I even *think* you've gotten off the couch for anything but a trip to the bathroom, I'm going to call security and tell them I'm being robbed. I'm going to scream bloody murder, and I'm going to cry. And they're going to believe every word."

"It's all coming into focus now."

She didn't like the tone of his voice. Or the smug look on his face. "What?" she asked, despite her better judgment.

"The real reason you made up Carter."

"I don't want to hear this. I really don't."

"I just hope you wrote down that number tonight."

"What number?"

"Your mother's psychiatrist." He moved close to her, backing her up against the wall. His hand moved toward her breast, paused, then fell back to his side. He looked at her again, smiled an evil Mitch smile. "He prescribes," he whispered.

He caught her hand before it could connect.

Chapter Seven

Mitch held her still, enjoying the feel of her as much as the fight in her. It was going to be so much fun to see her reaction when he got the scoop on Colker and she was left sitting in the dirt.

He'd only told her half the information he'd gotten tonight. Keeping it all to himself wouldn't have been fair. This way, the game would be more even. She did have a shot at finding out the truth—just not a very good shot. Unless, of course, Shelli got stood up by her boyfriend again, and Bentley was there to comfort her. Which didn't seem all that likely.

"Let me go, Slater."

"If I do, you'll hit me."

"I won't."

"I hear 'won't' on your lips, but I see 'will' in your eyes."

"What you see in my eyes is my heartfelt desire to strangle you. But that's illegal, so you don't have to fret."

"Fret? I don't fret."

"I think you should start."

"Bentley, what am I going to do with you?"

"Leave me. Abandon me. Take your things and go back to Los Angeles."

"Even if I wanted to go back, I can't now. Not with this weather."

"If you promise to leave, I'll change the weather. That's got to be easier to do than putting up with you."

"You're turning my head, you flatterer."

"Completely around, I hope."

"No wonder you don't have any friends."

"I do so."

"No you don't."

"How would you know?"

"I looked in your date book. The only numbers you have there are family and business."

"You *what?*"

She struggled some more, and he realized she was stronger than he'd thought. Maybe he shouldn't have mentioned that last thing. Live and learn.

"Let me go right now, you nosy, interfering, obnoxious son of a—"

"Bentley! I'm surprised at you. Such language from a lady."

"I'm not a lady."

"Honey, I've kissed you. I *know* you're a lady."

She got her left hand free and swung at him with a roundhouse punch. He ducked, of course, but he had to let go of her right hand, and then she was swinging again and coming too damn close, so he bent low, rushed forward, grabbed her around the middle and lifted her in the air. She was flung over his shoulder like a sack of wheat, only this sack had a great derriere that was patting close.

"Put me down. Right now. I'm calling the police. I'm going to scream. *Put me down!*"

He walked to the bed, really feeling her fists on his back, although she'd be even more steamed if he told her she was giving him a much better massage than his guy at the gym. Once he reached his target, he bent again and dumped Bentley unceremoniously on the bedspread.

He was just about ready to say something, but then he looked at her, all disheveled and pink, with that prim little skirt pulled up high on her thighs, and then he remembered her teddy, and he couldn't help wondering if that's what she had on under that white suit.

He felt a flush come on him suddenly, and his imagination went a little bonkers. He could see her, dammit, lying on the bed, wearing that teddy, looking the way she did right now, only she wanted him. As badly as he wanted her.

He felt himself harden, just like this afternoon. It must be the altitude, or the water, because he hadn't reacted this way around a woman since high school. Besides, it was Bentley lying there. The woman who alphabetized her canned food. Who cleaned her poker chips with Lysol. Who beat him out of the Russell story without so much as a by-your-leave.

She had gotten up on her elbows, the fury in her face making her somehow more beautiful, and soon she'd be standing again, ready for round two.

Nope. This boy was calling uncle. The last thing he wanted was for her to find out that Junior here, completely on its own without his permission, was getting ready to wake up and salute.

He turned and went to the closet, pulled down the extra blanket and unfolded it across the couch. It was a small couch, but he'd manage.

"What are you doing?" she asked, standing, fists curled, next to the bed.

"Going to sleep."

"Now?"

"It's late."

"But…"

"Yeah, that was fun, but it's time for beddy-bye. Go put on your jammies, kiddo. Get some shut-eye. It's going to be a big day tomorrow."

"But…"

"And turn off the light. Damn, listen to that wind out there, would you? I pity anyone out on a night like this."

With that, he curled himself into the most comfortable position he could, which ended up being about a three on a scale of ten, and closed his eyes. Unfortunately, the picture he'd conjured of Bentley on the bed still danced in front of him like a mirage. Sleep. The only cure was sleep.

Bentley stared at the ball of blanket on the small

couch. She didn't know what to do. First, she picked up the lamp on the nightstand, weighed it in her hands, calculated the probable damage to his hard head and realized it wouldn't inflict nearly the pain she was after.

She put it down and spied his belt hanging out of his bag. Wouldn't that be neat? Strangling him with his own belt? She took a step toward it, but then she thought about the police, and Stephanie's wedding, and what Babs would say, and she gave it up.

How did he do this to her? She'd never wanted to pummel anyone before. Ever. She was a gentle person. A sweet person. She gave money to Goodwill, dropped off presents in the Christmas barrel. Yet after less than twenty-four hours in the company of Mitch Slater, she was about an inch from committing a serious crime.

She saw him move a bit on the couch. At least he looked uncomfortable. It wasn't much, but it would have to do. Had she really thought, even for a second, that he was like her dream man? It must have been the alcohol or the stress or the water. There was a very good reason that she didn't like Mitch Slater. Several very good reasons. She wouldn't forget them again.

She turned from him, walked to the wall, turned off the light and went into the bathroom for a long, hot soak in the heart-shaped tub, and then bed.

THE KNOCK ON THE DOOR woke her. She sat up, confused from her dreams, and saw Mitch, wearing a pair of worn jeans and nothing else, let room service in. It was a large cart, and she could already smell the coffee. He took the check and signed it, and the waiter said, "Thank you, sir," and left.

Then Mitch poured a cup of java, put a little milk in it and brought it to her in bed.

"Light, no sugar, right?"

She nodded, awake now and suspicious. Why was he being nice to her?

He handed her the cup and saucer and sat himself down next to her. Again, she felt the dip of the mattress, felt his thigh against her thigh, only this time she moved over.

"How did you sleep?"

"Fine," she said. "Why?"

"Well, that's a nice good-morning."

"I dreamed you weren't here. Now you've spoiled it."

"Ouch."

"I'll say."

"Now, now. That's no way to start the day. I've thought about a lot of things this morning. I say we call a truce. Partners. Whoever gets the story shares it fifty-fifty. What do you say?"

She sipped the coffee, and it felt wonderful all the way down. The wind was still strong, but not as strong as it had been last night. She could see the clouds out there, swirling and huge, but they weren't all dark. A few of them were an almost silver white. "I say I don't trust you for a minute."

Mitch grabbed an imaginary arrow near his heart and yanked it out. "That hurt."

"You deserve worse."

"I know. But let's pretend, just for a minute, that I'm not the jerk you think I am. That I'm really here just to get a story, not destroy your life. That I figured we'd both be better off working as a team instead of going solo."

"That's asking a lot of my meager imagination."

"It's a big hotel, Bentley. And Colker isn't just going to open the door and offer us tea."

"He might. At least he might for me."

"You're cute, honey, but this is a man who's gone so far underground he doesn't need his eyes anymore. He's not going to fall for a pair of great legs."

She took another sip. "Great, huh?"

"Figure of speech."

"Thanks. So what do we do now?"

"I've been giving that some thought." He got up and walked over to the coffee and poured himself a cup. "I think this situation calls for the old divide and conquer. We figure out how to find Colker and get him to sit down for an hour or three for an interview."

She couldn't help but notice that his back was better than she'd ever suspected. She had a thing for backs. She liked them muscled, but not too muscled. Sleek, with that fabulous tapering that men did so well. Of course, it didn't hurt that his butt was just right, too. High, tight. She could bounce quarters off a butt like that.

He turned and came back to the bed. She knew she was blushing. She just hoped he wouldn't notice.

"Any ideas?" he asked.

She sipped first, then said, "How about we see if we can get some information out of room service. Take him his lunch?"

"Good. Isn't Babs doing some work with catering? Maybe she can tell us who's in charge."

"Getting Babs involved is dangerous."

"Not if it's done right."

"Let's hold up on that for a minute. First, let's give it a straightforward go. I'll go to the penthouse and see if I can make some headway. You can talk to Shelli again. See what else she'll tell you."

"Why don't I go upstairs—"

She glared at him. "I thought we were going to be partners."

"And so we are." He put his cup on the nightstand and stuck his hand out. "Partners."

She hesitated, but just for a second. She took his palm in hers. "Partners."

"So get dressed," he said. "We've got work to do."

"One more thing."

"Why do I feel like I should be worried?"

She put her cup down and leaned forward. "I need you to promise."

"Promise what?"

"That I can count on you to keep quiet about Carter." She waited for his reply, then noticed that he wasn't looking at her. His gaze had gone south. She looked down and saw that her nightgown, light cotton and very modest, was tucked into the covers and pressing against her breasts. It wasn't a big deal, for goodness' sake. She loosened the covers and adjusted her gown. Then she waved to get his attention. "Hello? I'm up here. If you want to talk to them, you have to ask permission."

He grinned and looked at her. "You didn't ask permission to peruse my butt."

"What? I did no such thing."

"I saw you in the mirror, doll. It normally doesn't take me more than a second to pour coffee. But you looked like you were enjoying the view so much, I dawdled."

She was going to have to learn how to stop this blushing thing. Her cheeks were hot, and she realized she'd blushed more in the last twenty-four hours than she had in her whole life. "So do you promise?"

"Huh?"

"About Carter."

"Ah. I won't promise never to tell, but I will do my best, as long as we're partners, to convince everyone I'm Carter."

"You think I'm going to go behind your back?" she asked innocently.

"I'm pretty sure it crossed your mind."

She sighed. "Fine. I can live with that."

"So? Why are you still in bed?"

She started to throw off the covers, until she saw that he was waiting, eyes ready, for a little skin show. "You need to do some dressing, too, cowboy."

"Can't blame a fellow for trying," he said, then turned to go to the closet.

Bentley got up quickly and put on her robe. Once she was decent, she selected her wardrobe for the day and took all she needed into the bathroom.

Her shower was a quick one, for her at least. And a disconcerting one. She couldn't escape the feeling of anticipation, of excitement that had her scrubbing a little too hard, smiling a little too much. She worked alone. Always had, always would, so what was the story here?

All right. If she had to tell the honest truth, she'd always admired Mitch. For his journalism. Not liked. Admired. So working with him was bound to teach her a thing or two. That had to be it. The eagerness she felt was the thirst for knowledge.

Completely satisfied, although still having random, unwelcome butt thoughts, she turned off the water and stepped out into her adventure.

MITCH WAS DRESSED and watching television when she left the bathroom. He was in a Hawaiian-style shirt, made more garish by the addition of prominent pink toucans liberally peppered over the garment. He was still in his jeans, and he'd put on tan canvas loafers to complete the ensemble.

She looked down at her beige tailored slacks and her subtly shaded beige-and-mushroom short-sleeved blouse and her spectator pumps. There was no way in hell she and Mitch were ever going to be able to work together.

She was scampi, he was fried shrimp. She was champagne, he was Ripple. It wasn't meant to be.

He heard her drop her hair blower on the dresser and turned. "Hey, you look sharp, as always."

"You look…colorful."

"I'll take that as a compliment." He pointed the remote at the TV. "Listen to this. We are having a hurricane, only we're just getting the edge of it. Bonnie. How dangerous could a hurricane named Bonnie be?"

"Exactly as dangerous as Hugo or Andrew."

"Nah. They're calling it moderate. A level two. And over here, we're just going to get a bit of wind and rain. Maybe a little flooding. A chance that the electricity will go, but only a chance."

"Did you ever get my batteries?"

"As a matter of fact, I did. They're right over there." He pointed, using the remote again, toward her suitcase, and she saw a crumpled paper bag.

She went for the bag, and her emergency supplies, which were in the left pocket of the case. Just as she reached out, someone knocked three times on the door. She veered right, to answer, but Mitch beat her to it. With his right hand, he opened the door—with his left, he took her completely by surprise and grasped her around the waist and pulled her toward him.

She gasped, had one second to see Babs standing in the hallway, and then she was being kissed.

The kiss was not moderate. It was intense, hot, fast and somehow sexier than it had any right to be. It was a French kiss, the kind she'd fought off in high school and longed for in college. It was deep and she felt swept away in a hurricane of her own.

"My goodness. I see you two have made up."

Her mother's voice changed everything, and she was back on the fourteenth floor, in her room. With her phony husband. She pushed him away, and he went, but not before giving her the single most lascivious smile she'd ever seen. Briefly, barely consciously, she squeezed her legs together at that smile. Then turned to Babs. "What's going on, Mother?"

"You sound like I interrupted something important. I can come back."

"No, Mom," Mitch said. "Come on in. Good to see you. Great of you to drop in."

Babs gave Mitch an odd look, then went immediately to the bed and sat on the edge. She gave the room a critical once-over, clearly disapproving of the clutter. If Mitch thought *she*, Bentley, was neat at work, wait till he got a load of the Immaculate Presentation over there. Babs's definition of clean was invisible.

"So, I finally got through to Stephanie. She's still in Honolulu, and she has no idea when she's going to get here."

Bentley moved over to the couch, prepared to sit for a long time while her mother recited her litany of woes.

"And I've yet to meet with the wedding coordinator. There are hundreds of things to do, and all your father can think about is his stomach. He ate waffles this morning. With butter and syrup. I swear, it won't surprise me if he has a heart attack right here. I shouldn't have left him alone in the room with the honor bar. He's probably eating peanuts as we speak."

Bentley nodded. It was really the only thing to do when Babs was on a roll. Just let her be, like a force of nature. No use fighting it.

She glanced at Mitch, who was trying to be polite and pay attention to her mother, but he was drawn to the TV. He kept trying to sneak peeks at the screen, then he'd catch himself and turn back, only to be enticed by the magic of the tube again.

It was his own fault. He was the one who wanted to be Carter. He sure kissed like Carter. Or like Carter would if he was real. She hadn't been kissed like that in years. Kissing was one of her favorite things in life, like cashmere and hot fudge sundaes. She hadn't known Mitch would be so good at it. Never suspected. But she was learning a lot about Mitch, wasn't she? How could she have worked with him for so long and been so oblivious?

It's because he was dangerous, that's why.

"...flowers are still in the truck, and thank God it's refrigerated, but for how long? Who knows. It's all going to fall apart...."

Bentley nodded once more. She was trying to listen to what her mother was saying, honest. But the combination of Babs's voice and the wind outside lulled her back to her own thoughts. Thoughts about Mitch.

What was she going to do about this partnership? Sure it sounded great, but this was Slater she was talking about. She watched him, smiling. He'd about given up the struggle and was watching the TV in earnest now. He didn't know that Babs didn't really expect anyone to pay attention. She just liked an audience.

"...five thousand dollars. And would you think she would wear the dress I picked out? Not a chance. She insisted on Oldham, when I told her La Croix was the only real wedding designer there was in..."

Trusting Mitch wasn't something a smart girl did. He was bound to double-cross her, it was practically genetic with him. So why had she agreed? Maybe she should do a little double-crossing on her own. Just in case.

"And it's Dinky this, and Dinky that. Your father roomed with him in college a hundred years ago, you'd think they'd be tired of each other by now...."

But what if he wasn't trying to pull a fast one? That would make her look like a first-class jerk. No. Everything she knew about Mitch warned her to be on her guard. Warned? There were practically neon signs shouting *Beware!* all over the room. Beware. Not just of the story. But of that kiss.

She was getting in over her head, and she'd better do something about that right now.

Chapter Eight

Bentley stood, stopping her mother midsentence. "It's great that you dropped in, Mother, but as you said, there are a hundred things to do. Why don't we—"

"But—" Babs looked at Mitch. "I thought—"

He shot up next to Bentley and grabbed her arm. "Why don't you offer Mom some coffee?"

She tried to pull her arm free, but he was gripping it tightly. Not enough to hurt, but she couldn't break free.

"What *is* it?"

"It's a hot beverage. Now, be nice and get her a cup." He smiled, then turned toward Babs. "So, tell me about the catering arrangements, Mom."

Bentley finally understood. Despite her request that Babs be kept out of things for the moment, Mitch was, as usual, doing whatever the hell he wanted. That had to be the shortest partnership on record.

"Really?" Babs asked, her voice almost trembling with gratitude. "You really want to hear?"

"Every word."

Bentley poured her mother a cup of coffee, handed it to her and turned to Mitch. She gave him an evil glare, which he seemed to think was a come-on, because he winked at her.

"We decided to go a bit native with the hors d'oeuvres. We've hired a sushi chef for the first hour, and we're bringing in dim sum carts. We'll also have…"

Bentley tuned her mother out. She'd heard the menu about a billion times, so that wasn't hard. She concentrated on Mitch, who was no longer struggling to keep his attention away from the television. As a matter of fact, he'd turned that off. Now it seemed that the struggle was between listening to Babs and keeping an eye on her.

She tested her theory by walking to the dresser. Yep, he followed her surreptitiously, just with his eyes and briefly at that. Why? What did he have up his Hawaiian shirtsleeve?

"Of course we have salmon for Danny. But we're also doing a filet mignon that…"

If she went into the bathroom and called for Mitch, would he come? Would he tell her what was going on? She doubted both. He clearly thought Babs had a way of getting to the room service people and that their plans from this morning were now history. What she couldn't figure out was why he had brought it up if he didn't want to be partners? He could have kept his mouth shut, and she wouldn't have suspected a thing.

Just then, there was another knock at the door. Three times, bam, bam, bam. Boy, it was like Grand Central Station in here. She crossed the room and reached for the knob.

In a startling repeat of his past performance, Mitch leapt over the edge of the couch, opened the door and swung Bentley into his arms. His kiss was a repeat, too. No. That wasn't right. It was more this time. More because she wanted it. Him. She felt her breasts press against his chest, his heartbeat rapid and urgent. Were they both insane?

She shoved him back and saw that it was her father at the door, and he'd witnessed the whole kissing business. Mitch turned to welcome him, but she caught his arm and pulled him back.

"What the hell is going on?" she whispered.

He blinked at her, straightened his back and somehow managed to look wounded and belligerent at the same time. "I'm just doing what you asked. Making sure your family believes I'm Carter."

"They believe. So knock it off."

"Geez, Bentley…"

"So I thought we were going to breakfast," Dan said. "I'm starving."

"You're always starving," Babs said. "Come in and sit down. I'm talking to Carter."

Mitch slipped from Bentley's grasp and joined Dan on the couch. "How you doing, Pop?"

"Very fine, Carter."

"Can Bentley get you some coffee?"

"Don't drink the stuff. I'm a juice man."

"Ah," Mitch said, staring at Bentley, smiling as if the whole thing were a colossal joke. "We were just talking about the wedding."

"Didn't look like it a minute ago. Looked to me like you two were half on your way to hitting the sheets."

"Daddy!" Bentley flushed, very surprised to hear her father talk like that. He never mentioned sex. Ever.

"You know Bentley," Mitch said, leaning back and adjusting his cushion. "She just won't leave me alone."

Danny laughed. Hard. As if that comment were a shared joke of long standing. She expected that kind of nonsense from Mitch, but not her father. How come he was so chummy with Mitch all of a sudden? And why did he feel so free to discuss her sex life?

"I thought you were hungry," she said, trying hard to will her parents into leaving. This whole morning was going wrong, yet nothing had actually *happened.* Mostly she felt as though everyone else had gotten a script to study, and she was forced to ad-lib.

"Come on and sit down, honey," Mitch said, patting the very small space next to him on the couch. "We're in no rush."

She started to tell him just where he could pat, but her folks had stopped talking, were staring at her, waiting for her to sit. "I've got to pick up," she said. "It's really a mess in here."

"That's what maids are for," Mitch said. "Come on. Don't be shy."

"I'm not shy. I just don't feel like—"

"Bentley," her mother interrupted as she stood. "Join me in the rest room, would you?"

She didn't want to. It made her nervous to leave Mitch out there with her father. Who knows what they would say? Probably discuss what she wore to bed. Or worse. But she followed. Babs could be insistent as hell, and Bentley was in no mood for a fight. At least not with her mother.

She stepped inside the small room, and Babs shut the door. Before she could say a word, her mother held up a stopping hand. "I know you're not comfy with this, but I just want to say it one more time. You must *try* with Carter, dear. He's a very lovely young man, and he's mad about you. I know he wants to make this trip special by having you conceive a child, which of course would make your father and me very happy, but that won't happen unless you loosen up. I read in *Cosmo* that stress is the number one cause of infertility among women your age, and if you don't snap out of this funk, or whatever it is, you'll never give me a grandchild, and that's just not acceptable."

Bentley knew her mouth was open, but she was too startled to shut it. She tried to think of something to say. Anything. How had her womb become the topic of the week? Why was she having this discussion with her mother? Why had she ever come to Hawaii in the first place?

"Promise me you'll make an effort."

"An effort?"

Babs nodded. "To be nice to him. To try."

"Why don't we just go at it now? Try to make things *special* and conceive that grandson while you're here? I'm sure room service would send up breakfast. It'll be cozy."

Babs crossed her arms. "You just have to run to that sarcasm, don't you?"

"I think the situation calls for a bit of sarcasm, yes."

"I'm only thinking of you."

"No, you're not. You're thinking of yourself. Just like always. If, and that's a very big if, I decide to have children, it won't be to satisfy your wish for a grandchild."

"You can be very cruel. Does Carter know that?"

"Not yet. But the day is still young."

"Stop it. I hate it when you get like this."

"Then let it alone, Mother. It's not your affair."

Babs sniffed, opened the door and walked out.

It wasn't Bentley's proudest moment. But she was

glad she'd put a stop to the grandchild business. It was all she seemed to hear about these days. Ever since she'd "married" Carter. Sometimes it felt as though her parents only wanted that from her. Nothing else. Just a precious heir, and of course, the trust fund.

The crazy thing was, she did want a child. Not as a gift to her folks, but for herself. She wanted a family, a nice house, a stable relationship. But not now. Her Pulitzer came first. And dammit, Colker just might be the one to give that to her.

A new determination swelled in her chest. She wasn't going to let them rule her life. Not Babs, not her father and certainly not Mitch. He didn't want a partnership? Fine. She liked working alone better anyway.

As for all that kissing—that would stop, too. It was all a joke to him. An amusing little parlor trick. Well, she was no dancing pony. She was flesh and blood, and she had feelings, too. If there was going to be kissing, she wanted it to matter. *She* wanted to matter.

She left the bathroom. Mitch and her father were still on the couch, and Babs was back on the edge of the bed. They all seemed to be having a dandy time. Mitch caught her eye, and while he started out looking cocky and smug, after a moment, his smile faded and he appeared concerned.

She went to the closet and started folding her nightgown, not willing to look at him. She hadn't asked for his concern. It was probably as phony as the rest of him.

"Excuse me," Mitch said as he stood and stepped over Dan's legs. Something had happened in that bathroom. Bentley looked as though she'd been through the wringer.

"Hey," he said, softly so only she would hear. "What's wrong? What did she say to you in there?"

Bentley turned to him. She'd never looked more patrician, more like the daughter of Babs and Danforth Brewster of Boston. Like a woman who wouldn't waste her time on a street rat like him.

"She didn't say anything I haven't heard before."

"Such as?"

Bentley put the folded gown down on the suitcase. "Even if we were married, which is an idea that makes me want to join a convent, it wouldn't give you the right to ask me that. Why is it that you people think my thoughts, and my body, are community property?"

"Whoa. Hold it right there." Mitch left her and joined her parents once more. "Why don't we join you downstairs," he said. "Give us a few minutes."

Babs nodded knowingly, and Dan looked pleased that he would be eating soon.

"Talk some sense into her," Babs said, touching his arm briefly and speaking in a whisper. "Sometimes the girl doesn't know what's good for her."

He nodded, but wished she hadn't said that to him. She was Bentley's mother. She should be on her side.

In a moment, they'd left. No goodbye to Bentley. Just one final look from Mom that told him a lot more than her words had.

"So, what's going on, partner?" He walked close to Bentley, who'd moved to the bed.

"Partner? Oh, really?"

"Sure. I thought we had that all worked out."

"We did. For about five hot seconds."

"What in hell are you going on about?"

She picked up a pillow, then threw it back on the bed. "Don't insult my intelligence," she said. "You think I didn't realize why my mother and father just happened to come by? That I didn't notice you couldn't wait to hear about the catering?"

Aha. Now he was starting to get it. "No, I don't think you do."

"No?" She turned on him with a blazing glare. "We are no longer partners, bucko. Not now, not ever. You have about as much integrity as a...as a..."

"Politician?"

"Don't you get cute with me. I'm too angry for cute."

"Nah. You can never be too angry for cute."

"I'm warning you. Knock it off. Better yet, just go. Just go find Darren Colker and get your story and win your Pulitzer and leave me the hell alone." Bentley swung around abruptly and headed for the bathroom.

Mitch raced her for it and won, blocking her entrance at the doorway. "You're all wet, snookems."

"Don't call me that. Oh, you are the most infuriating man I've ever met."

"Thanks, but let's not get off track. I didn't ask your mother to come up here to talk about the catering."

"Then why did you ask her?"

He reached behind her and knocked three times.

She furrowed her brow. "What?"

He did it again. Knocked three times. Then he took her by the waist and pulled her close. "This is why."

He kissed her. If that had been all, it would have been enough, but it wasn't. He ran his hand down her back, feeling the soft skin beneath her shirt. Her breasts pressed against his chest, and never before had he been so grateful for the differences between men and women. He tasted the faint hint of coffee and the sweetness of her mouth. More than all of that, he felt her respond. He felt her lean into him, conform to his hold. And when he brought his hand to her breast and cupped it softly, he felt her nipple stiffen and then he couldn't think anymore.

Bentley was surely going out of her mind. She should push him away, tell him to go to hell, not to touch her ever again. He was an intruder, a thief, a devil in jeans, but oh Lord, the way he kissed.

She'd never felt this way before. She'd never felt her blood run so hot, her skin be so sensitive. He had found a hidden switch in her and turned it on, and she wasn't sure she had the power to turn it off.

Not when his kiss deepened and she had to back up to get support from the wall because she'd lost her equilibrium as well as her senses.

She heard a moan and realized it was her own. Then another, but this time it was Mitch, and he was touching her all over, setting tiny fires that burned out of control.

She ran her hands over his back, picturing the beauty and the strength of him through closed eyes. The strength that was at the bottom of her need, the very core. His confidence, his potency, his absolute certainty about who he was and where he was going.

All those things swirled between them, and she felt drunk with them.

His hand moved down her stomach, and she shifted her body so he had free rein. He took his kisses and moved them to the curve of her neck, and she gasped with the pleasure.

It wasn't her, not her. She could never do this, not with him. He was Mitch, and he was so different in every way from any man she'd ever known. He was dangerous.

Dangerous.

She froze. "Wait a minute."

He didn't stop. His hands continued their exploration, and his mouth went on teasing her hot skin.

She moved her hands to his chest and pushed him away. "I said *wait.*"

"What?" His face was flushed, his dark hair tousled, and his eyes were still focused on her neck.

"You called them."

"Huh?"

"You called my parents to come here."

"Yeah? So?"

"You called them so you could kiss me."

He smiled, finally seeing her, shaking off the spell that had transfixed them both.

"Good plan, huh?"

She pushed him further away and walked out of the bathroom. "What the hell is this, Slater? A game? Let's score with Bentley as long as we're here?"

He followed her out, nearly on her heels. "No. I just—"

"You just what?" She turned to him and crossed her arms over her chest. "The partnership is a business deal, Mitch. Nothing more. It doesn't entitle you to conjugal rights."

"Hey, I wasn't the only person kissing in there."

She blinked. "You surprised me."

"The first time. There were no surprises in that bathroom just now."

"I was upset. It had nothing to do with you."

"Your nose just got longer, kiddo."

"I am not going to have this discussion with you. For God's sake, we work together. We have to go back to the office, and we're not going to be partners back there, remember? This is a onetime, never-to-be-repeated experiment, and that's it. Once we're back home, *kiddo,* you're the competition. Period."

"So? What does that have to do with anything?"

"Are you and I having the same conversation?"

He moved toward her and she backed up. Touching him was clearly the big thing to avoid. It wiped all clear thinking from her brain.

"I'm not asking you to get married here, Bentley. It's just a weekend. A great weekend, but that's it."

"That's all I am to you? A one-night stand?"

"Four nights, actually."

"What!"

"What? All I'm saying is that I'm here, you're here, and I have to say you look really great, we're already roommates, and damn, I kinda like you, Brewster. That's the kicker. I'm having a fine old time here. You're a big part of that. Besides, it's Hawaii."

She didn't believe what she was hearing. The nerve, the arrogance. It was all so out of bounds that she couldn't remember how to talk. Finally, after what seemed like five minutes, she shook away her amazement and could speak again. "You're unbelievable."

He grinned and straightened his back. "Thanks."

"That wasn't a compliment."

"Sure it was. You just don't know it yet."

"There is no way in hell I'm going to sleep with you, Slater. Got that? I don't care if you are having a fine time. It's not going to happen."

"Sure it is. You just don't know—"

"Stop." She went to the dresser and got her purse. "Don't say anything. I'm not going to listen to this for one more second."

"But—"

She covered her ears with her palms. "I can't hear you."

"Hold it."

She started singing. "This Old Man." Loudly. It worked. She didn't hear him anymore. She went to the door and exposed one ear as she reached for the knob. "This old man, he played—"

A knock, a big one, scared the wits out of her and she jumped back. Then came another knock. Then one more. She turned to Mitch.

"That should be Aunt Tildy," he said, grinning foolishly. "And Uncle Arthur is due in about five minutes."

"Kisses? You want kisses?" She flung the door open. There was Tildy, all right. The old woman stood there, sturdy as a tree trunk, her cane held aloft, ready to strike. Bentley noticed briefly that she'd forgotten her teeth again.

"There you go," she said to Mitch. "She's here. You're here. She likes you. Besides. It's Hawaii." With that, she swept past her startled aunt and walked away.

She heard his laughter all the way down the hall.

Chapter Nine

Now that she was in the lobby, Bentley wasn't quite sure what she was going to do with herself. It was crowded, like the night before, but this time there was an even greater feeling of tension in the air. Or was that just her?

No, the wind had picked up again, and since so much of the hotel was open-air, the staff had tied huge sheets of canvas around the entrance and, she discovered, around the bar. The rattle of the canvas was as disconcerting as the sound of the wind itself. It made her think of flapping sheets on a clothesline—a really big clothesline.

The natives were more than restless in the bar. Laughter splintered all around her; shards of noise whipped loudly past her, only to be swallowed in the wind. Bentley checked the area for family or friends. She didn't want either right now. She wanted a quiet spot, a cool drink, and it wouldn't hurt if her waiter was a cute cabana boy. But quiet was clearly out of the question. She even had serious doubts about the cabana boy. The cool drink, however, was just a matter of elbowing a few ribs to get to the bartender.

She went past several tables, then barreled into the packed crowd at the bar itself. It wasn't easy. Evidently, more than one man felt it was his duty to pinch her behind, and although she spun quickly—well, as quickly as she could with five bodies pressed against her—she didn't catch the culprits. She wished she had. It would be nice to have a reason to punch someone in the nose.

Finally, she got to the bar. It would be a wait, though, as the bartender was all the way on the other end making something in the blender. She kept getting pushed, hard, from behind. Her stomach was smashed flat, and her breath kept escaping in a whoosh. But she kept the vigil.

It was good to have so much going on around her. It kept her from thinking about what had taken place upstairs. For heaven's sake, what had happened to her? Why did she let him get to her?

In the three years she'd known Mitch, she'd never once thought of him sexually. Well, okay. Maybe once. Definitely not more than twice. Less than half a dozen times for sure. He wasn't her type. Not at all. He was aggressive and impolite and uncultured and boorish. He was the worst of all things: a great-looking man who knew he was a great-looking man. He walked around as if he could have any woman he wanted. Unfortunately, that was mostly true. What a sad commentary on her sex. How so many women could fall for his easy charm was a mystery to her.

Couldn't they see who he really was? That he was interested in a woman for one thing, and one thing only? The thought of Mitch Slater making a commitment was laughable. And marriage? He probably couldn't even go steady without breaking out in hives.

"What'll you have?"

Bentley looked up, startled by the bartender's shout. "Piña colada. Heavy on the colada."

He nodded. She put her purse on the bar and went looking for her credit card. Once it was in hand, she gripped it tightly.

The man next to her bumped her in the shoulder. It was the fourth time, and she was getting pretty tired of it. She needed to be alone. To think. To figure out how she was going to deal with her situation over the next few days. If she approached things logically, everything would be fine. She was sure of that. Logic and reason had saved her time and again.

She'd had a problem with all the suitors Babs had sent her way, and she'd dealt with that calmly and sensibly. She'd invented Carter. Perfect example. Now all she had to do was un-invent Mitch. Make him vanish.

Colker. She smiled. There was only one thing that would make Mitch butt out, and that's if he got the story. So what if she didn't get the Pulitzer on this one? It would be worth it.

"Here you go. That's six-fifty."

She took her tall glass, bedecked with a tiny paper umbrella, and gave the man her card. He wandered away and she sipped the drink. It was wonderful. As wonderful as her plan.

The bartender was quick, and business was done in a moment. Bentley shoved her way out of the pack without spilling a drop.

The tables were full. All of them except one, on the far side of the bar near the pool. She hurried, racing to claim the territory for America, and she made it. She was safe in her small space, and for the first time this morning, she relaxed.

But not for long.

"Hey, sweet cheeks."

It was Mitch. Scourge of the South Pacific. He turned a chair and sat, straddling the seat and resting his arms on the back. "That was some nice move up there. Aunt Tildy and I had a real good talk."

"Only talk?"

He nodded. "Seems I'm not her type."

"Tildy is a smart woman."

"She also has a great memory."

Something in her stomach tensed. He was far too chipper, too eager to chat. "I don't want to hear it," she said.

"You don't even know what I'm going to say."

"Let's keep it that way, okay?"

"Fine," he said, way too casually. "What's that you're drinking?"

"It's mine. You can't have any."

"But the crowd at the bar is ridiculous." He gave the room a cursory glance. "No waiters around. Don't you want to share a little with a poor, thirsty guy?"

"No."

He sighed, very dramatically. "I guess I'll never know if what Tildy told me is true or not."

"Oh, God. What?"

"Nothing. Just, you know, about Peter."

She straightened a bit in her chair while more of her insides tightened. "She told you about Peter?"

"Yep." Mitch flung his arms out wide and stretched while he looked once more at the crowd at the bar. Then he stood. "Guess I'll go stand in line."

"Oh, sit down." She pushed her drink at him. "Let's get it over with."

He did as she said, smiling a happy victory smile that she wanted to wipe off his face. It wasn't enough for him to take a polite sip of her drink. He gulped it like mother's milk, making moaning noises the whole time. When he put down the glass, he picked up his smile where he'd left off.

"Go on," she said. "I don't have all day."

"She told me about your motion picture debut. Pretty slick, snookems."

Bentley felt her cheeks start to warm. "It wasn't a big deal. I was young. In love."

"Right. It wasn't your fault there was a surveillance camera in the greenhouse." He leaned forward, evil glee lighting up his eyes. "Or that Babs and Danny were privileged to witness the deflowering of their eldest daughter. Only in black and white, but hey, you can't have everything."

"I wasn't deflowered."

"Hmm. That can go either way." He picked up her piña colada and took another great sip, leaving her close to nothing. "Evidently, the police officer claimed you didn't go all the way, but the people your folks had over for dinner—the Butlers, wasn't it?—said very confidently that you were no longer eligible to be thrown into active volcanoes."

Bentley folded her arms across her chest and gave Mitch her best stare. Despite the fire in her cheeks, she was not going to give him the satisfaction of knowing Tildy had told him her most humiliating moment ever. That she'd never gone into the greenhouse again, and that Peter, the boy she'd loved all through junior high and high school, had transferred to a military academy for his senior year. Or that her mother had taken her to the gynecologist the next day to get birth control, even though Bentley had sworn she hadn't gone all the way.

"Come on," he said. "Even you have to see the humor in this."

"No, actually, I don't."

He dropped his grin and studied her carefully for a moment. "Why not?"

"It wasn't funny. It was a horrible experience, and I was humiliated."

"But it's over. It's been over for, what, twelve years?"

"The memory lingers."

"That's your problem, Brewster. You don't know how to let things go."

"Thank you, Dr. Freud. But don't you have a story to steal?"

"Colker isn't going anywhere." He stood up and turned the chair around so he could scoot closer to her. Once he was settled he caught sight of a waiter and flagged him down. He ordered two more piña coladas, then faced her squarely.

"I don't want to talk about this," she said. "You're right. It did happen too long ago to matter. I think I'll skip the drink and go on up to the penthouse." It was her turn to stand, but Mitch grabbed her wrist.

"Don't. Just for a minute."

He didn't appear to have an ulterior motive. Even if he was Mitch, she'd never known him to be deliberately cruel. She gave in, knowing that if he started anything, she'd be out of there in a heartbeat.

"I'm sitting. Talk."

"Why is Babs so determined to get you pregnant? I mean, to see that you get pregnant."

"She wants an heir. For the money."

Mitch shook his head. "I don't buy that. Lots of mothers want their daughters to have babies, but with Babs it's like an obsession. That's what puzzles me. I mean, with other things, she's pretty normal. Pushy, but normal. This thing with a baby, though, that's odd.''

"Why do you care? It has nothing to do with you."

He looked startled. "Because it makes you unhappy."

His answer took her breath away for a moment, as if she'd been punched, nicely, in the stomach. But this was Mitch. Dangerous Mitch. She smiled as nonchalantly as she could. "*You* make me unhappy, but you still won't leave."

"You'd miss me if I were gone."

"Let me find out. Please."

He reached over and took one of her hands in his. "Off the record, I'm glad I'm getting to know you, kiddo. You're a real piece of work."

"Off the record, you're not quite as bad as I thought."

He made a face and sniffed. "I think I'm gonna cry."

She grabbed her hand back. "Okay. Fun's fun, but we have a story to get. I'm going up to the penthouse. You're going to find the delightful Shelli."

"We have drinks coming."

"That first one made me full." She got up again, more determined to leave than before. But for a totally different reason. "I'll meet you back in the room at one. Okay?"

"I'm synchronizing my watch."

"You're such a smart-ass."

"It's my job."

"You do it well." She left with the image of his smile on her mind. If she'd tried for a hundred years, she could never have anticipated that conversation. He'd caught her completely off guard. First with the Peter incident, but even more so with his observation about Babs.

Her mother *was* obsessed with having a grand-child. Sadly, the reason wasn't altruistic in any way. She might say she longed to spoil a baby again, but they all knew that was only a tiny part of it. She wanted an heir, not a grandchild.

It wasn't just with her, either. Stephanie was going through the same thing. Bentley didn't know for sure, but she suspected this wedding was Stephanie's way of appeasing Babs. She hoped not. She hoped Steph was marrying for love. Jack was certainly nice enough for that. But she'd never seen those kind of sparks between them.

But who knew? Things changed over the years. Maybe they'd been hit by Cupid when they least expected it.

Regardless, that didn't change anything about this weekend. As long as Mitch was here, the pressure to have a baby wouldn't let up. Not unless she did something to stop it. But what? How could she possibly deal with the baby issue while her hands were full with Mitch? It didn't seem fair, and for once she was going to do a Scarlett O'Hara and think about her mother problems tomorrow.

In the meantime, she wanted to find Colker. To get Mitch his story so he'd leave her be. So she could have her life back. Her safe, predictable life.

First stop was the front desk. A pretty brunette was manning the station. Four people stood waiting for her attention, and the girl looked flustered. Bentley got in line.

While she waited, she tried to read the girl's name tag. She'd have bet the farm it read Shelli. The girl looked like someone Mitch could charm. Young, innocent and not too bright. Perhaps that was unfair. Just because Mitch liked her, it didn't necessarily follow that she'd be dumb. It was just likely.

Moving forward as two people left the scene, Bentley was finally able to read her gold name tag. Shelli it was. The reporter's instinct was a powerful force. She must remember to use it only for good.

It was her turn next, and she needed to stop congratulating herself on her keen intelligence and figure out what she was going to ask. She couldn't just blurt out that she wanted to find Darren Colker, so could she please have his room number, and while you're at it, how about a key? But she could, maybe, find out which penthouse was his.

"Yes, ma'am?" Shelli said sweetly when Bentley reached the polished wood counter. "Can I help you?"

Bentley recognized a hint of a Southern accent. Georgia, or maybe Louisiana. Definitely not south Hawaii.

"I hope so, sugah," Bentley said, glad that she'd played Blanche Dubois in college. "I'm interested in your suites. Penthouse suites."

"I'm afraid we don't have any available right now, Miss"

"Beauregard. Beulah Beauregard, of Baton Rouge."

Shelli smiled brightly. "Why, I'm from Louisiana. Lake Charles."

"Honey, I knew you looked like a hometown girl. Now, about those suites…"

"Honest, Ms. Beauregard. We're fully booked—"

"I don't need one right now, sugah. I'm thinking of next month, when I come back to this little island paradise with my new husband. He won't stay anywhere but in the penthouse, darlin'. And I have no intention of disobeyin' his desires."

"Well, we have three penthouse suites. Two run at twelve hundred a night, and one is fifteen hundred."

"That's all you have? Three?"

Shelli shook her head and her long brown hair swung prettily over her shoulder. "No, ma'am. We have four. But one is a permanent residence."

"You don't say. I think that's a very wise idea, actually. Why bother renting a room, risking that someone else has beaten you to the punch, as it were. I'd like to see that penthouse, if I may."

"I'm sorry. I can't show you. Someone lives there."

"I'm sure if you called and explained the situation, he wouldn't mind at all. It would be a common courtesy."

"Oh, no. Not with Mr.—this guest. He wouldn't like that at all."

"Do you have another suite just like his?"

"Yes, ma'am. Number 1602 is identical in every way."

"May I see that room?"

Shelli shook her head, but this time no hair flew. "I can't do that right now. Not when it's occupied."

Bentley leaned over the counter, signaling Shelli to come close. Meanwhile, she dug into her purse and prayed she'd remembered to put her emergency hundred in the secret flap.

"What time do y'all send up your cleaning crew to room 1602? Maybe I could catch a little, itty-bitty peek then." She folded her hand around the bill, brought it to the desk and slid it surreptitiously to Shelli.

She knew Shelli had recognized the denomination when her eyes opened very, very wide. Then Shelli looked around, presumably to see if any staff were within earshot. The coast must have been clear, because Shelli leaned forward, too, and whispered, "Three-fifteen. Except on Tuesdays. Then it's four."

Bentley straightened and gave Shelli a warm, thankful smile. "Sugah, you do the South proud. You be good, y'hear?"

Shelli put the bill in her jacket pocket. "I'll do my best, ma'am."

Bentley turned, anxious to get up to the penthouse. It was only noon, so the cleaning crew wouldn't be up there for a few hours yet, but she wanted to make certain she knew where she was going when the time was right. She glanced once more at her watch as she walked toward the elevator.

She didn't make it. Once again, Mitch was in her way. Talk about a bad penny. "What are you doing here?" she said. "Shelli's at the front desk."

"Well, shut my mouth, Lulabelle," Mitch drawled in a terrible Southern accent. "You didn't tell me you were a rebel. I thought you were a Yankee, and you know how our people hate those damn Yankees."

"I don't have time to talk baseball with you, Slater. I have successfully completed half my mission. How about you?"

"Lawzee, Ms. Beauregard. I don't know nothin' 'bout completin' no mission."

"You have no business mocking me for masquerading as someone other than myself, *Carter*."

"Ah," he said, using his own voice again. "You've got me there."

"No. I've got you here. I want you there."

"Fine, fine. I'm leaving. But I can't do anything until Shelli gets off work. And you can't do anything until the cleaning crew arrives. So why don't we do it together."

"Good idea. Let's go surfing. I'll meet you in the water."

Mitch laughed a big old fake laugh. "You are just so *cute* when you tell me to go to hell. I could listen to it all day."

"Listen and learn. Now leave me alone. I have work to do."

"What kind of work?"

"That's none of your business."

Mitch opened his mouth, but before he could utter a sound, she'd put her hands to her ears and began singing a reprise of "This Old Man." She didn't even care that all the people near her turned and stared. She just walked to the elevator, singing that old song as if she were Ella Fitzgerald herself.

Mitch watched her enter the elevator and let loose with the laughter he'd been holding back. Now the good people who'd stared at Bentley turned to stare at him. He couldn't have cared less. He was having too damn much fun.

He had been telling her the truth a minute ago. He didn't want to go his separate way. It was hard to believe, given his track record, that he liked working with a partner, but there you had it.

Bentley made him think. She also made him laugh. A mighty big duet in his book. He'd always settled for one or the other in a woman, and now he'd found both. In the delightful package of his partner. How about that.

Not that he wanted to make the arrangement permanent. God forbid. He worked alone, played the field and owed no debt to man or beast. He'd learned early to trust only one person—himself. Other people flaked out on you, no matter how badly you needed them.

Turning his back on the elevator, he caught sight of Shelli leaving her post. He hurried that way, wondering if she was just going to the office on some business matter or if it was, in fact, her shift change.

When he got there, another clerk was manning the desk. Shelli hadn't come out, so he had to assume she was off. And that she was probably going to leave the hotel.

He walked to the right until he found a door marked Private. It wasn't locked, no reason for it to be, so he went inside.

There was a hallway with three doors off to the side. Walking past the first doorway, he glanced inside a small office and spied a computer on the desk. No one was in there, and the sign on that door said Manager. Checking once to make sure he was alone, Mitch slipped inside the room and shut the door behind him.

The computer was running. It showed some kind of database. There were names running down the left column. Guest names? Wow, yes, there were room numbers three fields away. He started hitting the Up arrow, trying to race past the lower letters of the alphabet before someone walked in.

He'd reached the Ds when he heard someone at

the door. He searched for a place to hide, saw none
and ducked under the desk just in the nick of time.

It was a wide desk, and he had a bit of maneu-
vering room, but not enough. If the manager sat
down, he would kick him in the side in a minute.
The full impact of his lunacy hit him then, and he
almost started laughing. It was torture to hold it back
when he tried to imagine how he could explain all
this. God, they'd send him to jail. Or worse.

The someone in the office walked toward him. He
could make out footsteps, but only barely with the
thick carpet. Then he caught sight of some legs, and
he let out a mighty sigh of relief. Shelli. He'd recognize those legs anywhere.

He started to leave his cubbyhole, when the door
opened and closed for a second time. Keeping still
as a mouse, he waited, praying for visitor number
two to get the hell out. Instead, another pair of legs
joined Shelli. Man's legs.

"I couldn't wait to get you alone," the man said.

Then the legs got very close together. Front to
front. And the sounds followed shortly thereafter.
Kissing sounds. Moans. Gasps. The full gamut in the
making-out series of noises, so popular these days
with the young people.

He closed his eyes and tried to block out their
voices, but it was no good. He could hear them really
well. It didn't take long, however, for the noise issue
to become secondary to the pain-in-the-back issue.

He was in a hunched-up little ball, and he hadn't

done that since early childhood. It wasn't comfy. The pains had started out dull, but now they were moving up several notches to burning. Soon, they would be agonizing.

All this, and he'd only gotten up to the Ds.

"Mr. Marshall is out for lunch," Shelli said. "He won't be back for another half hour."

"I locked the door," the man said between slurping noises.

"Take me," Shelli said breathlessly. "Take me now."

Mitch moaned. Quietly. Shelli's friend clearly was taking her at her word, because her legs went up in the air, and he heard her perch on the edge of the desk. Then, her legs spread.

Mitch closed his eyes. And wished like hell that he knew the words to "This Old Man."

Chapter Ten

Bentley tried very hard to concentrate on Darren Colker. More specifically, what she was going to do with him once she got to the sixteenth floor. She needed this time to figure out her strategy, to have a plan and a fallback position.

Instead, she just kept thinking about Mitch.

At least she'd been granted a small grace period. The elevator seemed to stop at every floor, and someone inevitably cried, "Hold that elevator," so the wait was even longer.

The chatter inside was all about Hurricane Bonnie, of course. From what Bentley gathered, the winds were classified as moderate, with sustained gusts of about ninety miles per hour at the heart of the storm, but only about sixty miles here. Several men, meteorologists, she gathered from their confidence and knowledge, said the only way to get through a hurricane like this was to get completely soused, concentrating on rum drinks. Damn, there were no rum drinks in her emergency packet. What had she been thinking?

She smiled as the weathermen went on about being prepared, but the distraction only lasted another moment. Soon enough she was thinking about Mitch. Mostly about the look on his face when he'd said, "Because it makes you unhappy."

She'd been dwelling on that for a while, trying to see if she'd misinterpreted his words. Or if he'd only acted concerned, the way he'd acted interested in Babs's catering dilemmas.

The truth was, she had no idea. None. He'd sounded sincere. Looked earnest. But with Mitch, could she trust her instincts?

They stopped at the fourteenth floor, and she prayed that none of her family would board. Luck was with her, and she stayed among strangers.

What if his feelings were genuine? That he really did give a damn about her, and not just because of the story? Surprisingly, she wasn't totally sickened by the idea. He did know how to kiss. A very important attribute, that. Many flaws could be overlooked for excellent kissing. Many, but not all.

First, she had set her life goals, her road to success. Mitch was not in that scenario. Even if she was to veer off the straight and narrow, he would be the last person in the world she'd do it for. She needed a Carter. Not a Mitch. Carter was stable, solid, reliable. Slater was a disaster waiting to happen.

So why the angst? More important, why was her

body so damned perky whenever she was in his arms? Maybe she had a split personality. Yeah, right. She should be so lucky.

The elevator stopped, and she noticed that not only was she alone, but she'd reached the sixteenth floor and she had absolutely no idea what she was going to do.

She could take another round trip, but that seemed cowardly. Instead, she stepped into the hallway.

It was different up here. Not just the decor. The air seemed purer, the dust shamed away from this high-income bracket. The carpet was also more plush, she realized as she walked toward room 1602 and the maid's cart parked by the door.

It occurred to her that the wallpaper, a stunning, elegant flower print, would look fabulous in her bedroom. Of course, her furniture would then look like Salvation Army rejects, but it would be worth it to wake up to this every morning.

The sound of a vacuum cleaner caught her attention. Taking it slow, she walked toward it, praying that her journalistic instincts would burst out in a fit of brilliance to make up for her lack of strategy.

She found 1602, and across the hall 1600. If she was a betting woman, she would have wagered that 1600 belonged to Darren Colker, mystery billionaire.

Both doors were closed, and the cart was stationed closer to 1600 than its twin. She listened for the vacuum but heard nothing. Either someone had opened a door briefly or they'd finished with the carpets.

Summoning her courage, she knocked on 1602. The wait seemed interminable, but she didn't knock again. She took the time to berate herself for being yellow. If she had any guts at all, she'd bang on the door until someone answered, bully her way in and find out once and for all who lived up here. Clearly, guts were not listed in her personal inventory.

Just as she was about to leave, the door swung open. It wasn't a maid standing there. It was a man. Not Darren Colker. This was a younger man, and considerably better looking. Blond, tan, athletic, he reminded her of one of those boys in old movies who tied sweaters around their necks and asked, "Anyone for tennis?"

"It's about time," Golden Boy said, but not impatiently. He stepped back and gestured for her to come inside.

Bentley did, and she was immediately drawn toward the windows. She heard the door click shut behind her, but she couldn't turn away from the view. The walls on two sides were glass, and the view she got of the wild skies was simply overwhelming. It was dark and light, and clouds raced by in fast forward. It was *weather* like she'd never seen it before. She could watch it for hours and never lose interest.

When Golden Boy's hand grabbed her behind, however, she did lose interest. Fast. She twirled on him, shocked out of her mind. Who the hell had he been expecting?

"The bedroom's over there," he said. "You want a drink first?"

Bentley shook her head while she measured the distance between her and the door.

He gave her a critical once-over and nodded after he'd reached her feet. "Not bad," he said. "Classy. I like that. We can do headmaster and the tardy schoolgirl."

"We can what?"

He smiled. "I like that, too. Innocence itself."

Bentley started toward the door. This was way too weird, even for her. "I'm not who you think I am," she said. "I'm sorry I bothered you. I'll just be going now."

He went for her wrist and she darted behind a wing chair.

"I'm not her. I swear. I just made a mistake in room numbers. I'm looking for Mr. Colker."

"I'll be anyone you want, baby. Mr. Colker it is."

She made it halfway to the door before he intercepted from the right. She deflected, moving as quickly as she could, and placed herself between the couch and the man.

He just laughed and started to undo his belt.

"I'm going to call the police if you don't let me out of here this instant."

"Honey, I paid for you to struggle, but not this much. Wait till we're in the bedroom, okay?"

"No, no, no. I'm not a call girl. I'm a reporter. If

you'll just wait a second, I'll prove it. I've got a press I.D.''

"You want to change the game, huh? Okay, I'll be the editor and you can be the naughty copy boy. Girl. That's a new one. I like it.''

Bentley thought about screaming, but something about Golden Boy told her he was telling the truth, that he'd mistaken her for a call girl. "Look, Mr.—''

"The name's Peter.''

"Of course. Look, Peter. There really has been a mistake here. I don't know how you hired your...friend, but if you call and check, you'll see I'm not her.''

Instead of doing that, he unzipped his pants, pulled them down and stepped out of them. He was wearing leopard-skin briefs. His legs were actually quite good.

"I'm a guest at this hotel,'' she said, backing away, trying to get around him to the front door. "I even have a key. I'm here for my sister's wedding. Call the front desk, they'll tell you.''

Peter smiled as he unbuttoned his shirt. "What's your name, sweetheart?''

"Bentley. Bentley Brewster. Out of Boston. Currently living in Los Angeles. I'm a reporter for the *Times.*''

"Yeah, uh-huh. Look here, Bentley. I'm up for however you want to play this, but it can't take all day, you know? I've got some people to meet in about an hour. So can we speed this along?'' He took off his shirt and let it fall where he stood.

"I'm not playing, dammit. I'm not your hooker. And I'm leaving right now. If you try and stop me, I'll have you arrested for assault. Got it? This is not a joke.''

He looked her over once more. "You're not one of Sam's girls?''

Bentley sighed, grateful that her instincts had served her well. "No. I'm not.''

"So what do you say we go for it anyway? I'll pay you double.''

She made a beeline for the exit. "No. I don't think so.''

"No? I like that editor thing. You'd have a good time. I swear.''

"I'm sure you're just dynamite in the sack, Peter, but I've got some things to do.'' She took one final glance at the gorgeous sky, then opened the front door. Before she left, she turned to him. "Peter?''

He looked at her hopefully.

"Who lives across the way?''

His hopes dashed, he just shrugged. "Some old guy. Small. Doesn't say much. I've only seen him once or twice.''

"Thank you.'' She walked into the hallway but stuck her head in one more time. "Peter?''

"Yeah?''

"Just exactly how much is double?''

"A cool grand, Bentley Brewster. Care to reconsider?"

"Wow. How come you need to, you know...? You're quite a good-looking fellow."

He smiled a little sadly. "I'm also a rich fellow, and you'd be surprised how complicated that makes things."

"No, actually I wouldn't be surprised at all. Good luck."

"You, too."

She shut the door behind her.

MITCH HOBBLED OUT out of the manager's office exactly forty-five minutes after he'd entered. The most excruciating forty-five minutes of his life. Not only was his back killing him, but it had been pure torture listening to Shelli and Tiger have at it. He thought about leaving a note for the manager, telling him to be sure and lock his door when he was at meetings, but it was far more important to get the hell out of there.

Of course, he'd taken five minutes to continue perusing the database. He'd found a Mr. "C" in the penthouse. Room 1600. He was a permanent resident, and Mitch figured he'd found Colker. Although frankly, by the time he'd found Colker, he didn't give a damn. He just kept thinking about that big old Jacuzzi tub in the room.

He got to the elevator without moaning too loudly and silently cursed every person who pressed a number lower than fourteen. He survived the ride and made it to the room, sorry that Bentley wasn't inside. Kvetching was always better with an audience.

After turning on the water in the tub, he went to the window and stared at the sky. He wanted to be out there. To feel that wind on his face. After the bath, he just might go for a walk. That would clear out the cobwebs.

He needed something to shake him up. Get him back on track. The whole time Shelli and Tiger were boinking, he had been thinking about Bentley. Not about the story, like he should have, not about the sex being practiced above him, which also would have made sense. No. He was thinking about his partner. Then about his aching body then right back to Bentley.

She was a surprise. So was her family. Sure, they were dysfunctional. It wouldn't be normal if they weren't. But they were really a family. He liked the way they talked to him like one of their own. That was something new, something he'd not thought much about because he never expected it to happen.

Aunt Tildy was maybe his favorite. What an old trooper. She told him what she thought without any sugar coating. She'd also warned him to be good to Bentley. She even threatened to come back and haunt him after she died if he didn't treat her favorite niece right. Thatta girl, Tildy.

It wasn't hard for him to understand why Bentley was her favorite. He'd never met Bentley's sister, and he was sure she was very nice indeed, but she was no Bentley. No way there could be two.

Mitch went to the bar and pulled out a beer, then went in to check on the tub. It was a big tub, and only halfway full. Too bad. He shucked his clothes, leaving them in a heap on the floor, and eased himself into the hot water. He moaned happily, then laughed when he realized he sounded just like Tiger. About five minutes into this afternoon's entertainment, he'd decided that if any woman ever called him Tiger at a critical moment, he'd deflate like a popped balloon.

He settled himself advantageously in front of a well placed jet, took a long slug of beer and closed his eyes.

Bentley sitting next to him would have made everything perfect. If he couldn't have her in person, he'd settle for a dream.

BENTLEY OPENED THE DOOR to her room, half expecting Mitch to be waiting. When she found herself alone, she felt more than a little disappointed, which was crazy, as she most decidedly wanted him out of her life.

She tossed her purse on the bed. She wanted to jot down some notes about her experience upstairs. It was too funny, and she had the feeling it would make a great column. But more than that, she wanted to tell Mitch. She wanted to casually repeat the amount of money she'd been offered and see his reaction. He would make jokes, but it would also sink in that she was not an off-the-rack item.

As she looked for some paper, she wondered how he was doing with Shelli. Was he hoping to get information from her in a less-than-honorable fashion? Probably. Bentley didn't want to think about how many stories Mitch had gotten in the bedroom. She'd seen the pen he always carried. The one that wrote upside down. Bet that came in handy.

The only paper she could find was the hotel stationery. It would do. She sat at the desk and started writing, but her concentration wasn't so hot. She needed to freshen up, throw a little cold water on her face.

Something slammed against the window, and she jumped, but nothing was there when she went to investigate. Probably a tree limb or something. Her view, wonderful as it was, was dwarfed by good old Peter's. Maybe later she could... No. She was *not* going up there again, unless it was to interview Colker.

Sighing with sudden melancholy, she kicked off her shoes and headed for the bathroom. If only Mitch was here now. She would tell him about her adventures, and he'd say something horrible that would secretly tickle her to no end.

She opened the door and went to the sink. Using only cold water, and letting it run a second to get even cooler, she bent down and splashed her face. Once wasn't enough, but after three dashes, she felt better. Dripping wet, she turned and reached for a towel. It was fresh from the laundry, and it smelled surprisingly good for a hotel—

"Hi there, snookems."

Bentley dropped the towel, jumped back, hit her head against the shower door, tried to scream, couldn't do it, turned around twice until she found Mitch in the tub.

Naked.

She turned away, her face crimson. There hadn't been bubbles. It was a Jacuzzi, wasn't it? So where were the damn bubbles?

"Care to join me?" he said. "I can rev up the old motor in a hot second. It feels real good."

"I'm sorry. I didn't know... I didn't realize..."

"It's no big deal. I'm sure you've seen a naked guy before. Or didn't Peter take off his clothes?"

She swung around. "I'll have you know he offered me a thousand dollars."

"Wow. No wonder he joined the military academy. He couldn't afford a second shot at you."

"Not *that* Peter."

"There's another Peter?"

"Of course. I wouldn't have accepted money from *my* Peter."

"But you would from the other Peter."

"Of course not. What kind of a woman do you think I am?"

"Confused."

"I'm not the one talking about the wrong Peter."

"Bentley. Sweetie. I think you should just get out of those clothes and climb in next to me. You'll feel a lot better, and maybe you'll even make sense."

"Oh, sure. I suppose you wouldn't offer me double. No, not you. Not Mitch Slater. You would probably offer half."

"Uh-huh. Well, as much fun as this has been, I'm getting a little chilly. I think I'll just get out of the tub now."

Bentley, still steamed that he'd scared her like that, and more steamed that she'd told him about her adventure and all he'd done was get it wrong, tried to think of something snappy to say.

"Well?" he said.

"I'm thinking! Wait."

"Suit yourself."

The sound of the water splashing against the sides of the tub jerked her attention that way, and then she saw that Mitch hadn't waited at all. He was standing in the middle of the tub, dripping from every possible surface, smiling as if this were a normal way to spend an afternoon.

She couldn't help it, of course. She gazed right at the heart of the matter. Not that she wanted to, naturally. But it was some kind of magnet or something.

"Bentley?"

She nodded. "Yeah?"

"Finished?"

She dropped her head in her hands. Could this day

become any more embarrassing, or had she reached the very top of the humiliation scale. "Oh, God."

"No, just me. And I told you, I was getting cold."

She turned and fled, wanting to flee to mainland China but settling for the bed. Under the covers. Where she could experience her shame alone.

If she prayed hard enough, Mitch would leave her be. He would go somewhere far away. Another country. Another dimension. She wasn't particular.

Instead, she felt him sit on the bed. Had he gotten dressed? Had there been time? If he was naked, she didn't know what she was going to do.

"Bentley."

"Go away."

"Come on out, kid. It's okay. I'm not embarrassed."

"I am."

"Why? We're both adults."

"I'm immature for my age."

He tugged a bit on the comforter above her, but she hung on tight. No way she wanted to face him. Or his... Not like this.

"Bentley?"

"She's left the building."

"Whoever you are in there, I'm decent. Dressed. It's safe to come out."

She moved the covers down, slowly, until she could peek over the top. He was telling the truth. He'd put on his jeans.

She lowered the covers some more, still embarrassed beyond belief.

He smiled at her. "Well, that was interesting."

"Fascinating."

"Thank you."

"I didn't mean—"

He winked at her. "Sure you did. You just don't know it yet."

Chapter Eleven

"So, you want to tell me what happened?" Mitch had to struggle to keep the grin off his face. Bentley, the woman he'd seen take on Nelson Richardson single-handed, was still as flustered as a schoolgirl. It was kinda cute, actually. Endearing. Of course he couldn't tell her that. She'd sock him.

"I found out where Colker lives," she said, her voice still timid. She hadn't let go of the covers yet, although they'd gone from her chin to her chest.

"Yeah?"

"Room 1600. He doesn't come out much. He's small. The maids have already been there today, though, so we have to wait till tomorrow to do anything."

"Not necessarily." He stood up and went to the phone. After he punched the numbers for room service, he turned back to Bentley. "Come on. Get up. We've got work to do."

She looked at him with that cocker-spaniel head tilt of hers, but someone had answered the phone.

"Room service."

"What's your soup today?"

"Chicken noodle," the woman said.

"Send some up to Mr. C, please. Room 1600."

"Right away."

Mitch hung up the phone, relieved that there had been no secret password other than the use of the initial.

"What's going on?" Bentley said. She'd thrown off her covers and now sat at the edge of the bed, sliding her shoes on.

"I found out that his alias is Mr. C. Like in *Happy Days*. Original, eh?"

"Shelli told you?"

He smiled. "Not exactly." He went to the closet and grabbed a shirt, threw it on, then he slipped his shoes on, too. "I'll tell you about it sometime. But right now, I need you to tell me the layout of the sixteenth floor. Is there somewhere to hide while we wait for room service?"

Bentley didn't say anything for a minute. She just went to the mirror and combed her hair. He knew she was thinking, but he still fought the urge to prompt her.

He needed to get on with the search for Colker. After Bentley's impromptu appearance in the bathroom, he'd done nothing but think about what he wanted from her. It wasn't information.

He wanted *her*. More than he would have ever guessed. He'd considered that he might just be in a general state of horniness after his X-rated audio treat, but when he tried to picture any other woman in his arms, he couldn't do it.

He didn't want sex. He wanted to make love to Bentley. And since he doubted she would cheerfully agree, he had to keep his mind occupied and his body busy. So the Colker fortress was about to be stormed.

"I didn't see anywhere to hide," she said. "There are only two rooms on that side of the building."

"Okay. So scratch that. We'll have to create a diversion, but we'll also have to have an alibi."

"Peter. I can say we were up there to see him."

Mitch sat down on the couch. "This, I presume, is the other Peter?"

She nodded. "I'll tell you about it sometime."

"How do you know he won't be there to blow the deal?"

"He told me he had a meeting. But we'd better hurry because I have no idea how long it's supposed to last."

"You ready?"

"As I'll ever be."

Mitch stood and opened the door. "Let's hit it, partner."

The smile on her face did more for his general well-being than the Jacuzzi had. She looked eager and happy. Not just because they were going out sleuthing, but because they were sleuthing together.

He was pretty damn happy about that himself.

THE PLAN WOULD HAVE worked. It was a good plan, a reasonable plan. Only he hadn't factored in Bentley's mother.

It started the moment they stepped into the hall. Mitch had just shut the door behind him when he heard the unmistakable voice of Babs Brewster calling, "Yoo-hoo! Carter! Bentley! Over here!"

Bentley looked at him with resignation. He grabbed her hand and squeezed it, then whispered, "We'll get out of this. Trust me."

She shook her head. "Forget it. It's like trying to escape from Darth Vader. It won't happen."

"Just call me Luke."

"I'm so glad we found you," Babs said as she came within talking distance. "You didn't show up for breakfast. You didn't call me back. If I didn't know better, I'd say you were trying to avoid me."

"Mother, we've been busy. It wasn't intentional."

"Busy? With what?"

Bentley gave Mitch a look, sort of like a man on death row would give to his priest. "We're doing a story. Carter and I."

"On what? Hurricanes? Weddings that go to hell in a handbasket? Daughters driving their mother insane?"

"No. There's someone here we want to interview."

"You're on vacation. Your family should be your first priority, or is that simply too old-fashioned for you?"

Mitch watched the interplay between Bentley and her mother with new eyes. Now that he was beginning to understand a little about Bentley, he could see that her mother's influence was a powerful one, and that her move to Los Angeles, her job, her marriage to Carter had all taken a strength that most of the people he knew didn't have. Faced with a woman like Babs, ordinary folks would fold. Not Bentley. Even now she stood straight and tall, determined not to let the guilt win.

''Is there something you want me to do, Mom? Or do you just want to talk?''

''Talking is helping. You think it's easy for me, with Stephanie about to miss her own wedding? Your father doesn't care. He's watching sports with Arthur up in the room. Tildy is parked in her room and says she won't come down until she's sure the winds won't come through the canvas in the lobby. Evelyn Howell arrived, but who knows where she is. Dinky is allergic to shellfish, so we have to order a special meal for him. Francie and the boys—''

''Mother,'' Bentley interrupted. ''I'm sorry no one is there for you right now, but Mitch and I have some work to do. Tell you what. We'll do dinner together. I promise.''

''Mitch?''

Bentley froze. Mitch stared at her hard, wondering if he should step in now or if she could figure a way out of this.

"I meant Carter. The story we're doing, it's about Mitch Peterson."

"Who's that?"

"No one you'd be interested in."

Babs pressed her lips together, and Mitch could practically see the steam coming out of her ears. But he was damned impressed by Bentley's calm under pressure. No wonder she was such a good reporter.

"So, do you want to have dinner with us tonight?" Bentley asked.

"That's all I'll get, correct?"

"For today, yes."

Babs nodded, but it was a hard-given acknowledgment.

"Seven o'clock, same place as last night?"

Again, Babs nodded.

Bentley moved closer to her mother and touched her arm. She smiled gently and said, "The reservations will be in Daddy's name?"

It worked, sort of. Babs didn't smile back, but she softened. "Go get your story, if that will make you happy."

He didn't know why, but he went over to Babs and gave her a hug. It was a real one, not part of the charade. At first she was stiff as a board, but he kept on until she hugged him back. "We'll see you tonight, okay, Mom?" he said.

She patted his hand. "Go on. Get the elevator."

He took Bentley's hand and walked with her down the hall. "That was impressive," he said.

"She is a force to be reckoned with."

"I meant you."

She stopped. "Me?"

He pulled her forward again until they reached the elevator. He pressed the up arrow, then turned to her. "Yeah, you. You held your ground back there, but you did it with real class."

She studied their hands, linked together with ease, and he could guess what she was thinking. How did this happen? To the two of them, of all people?

Finally, she looked up. "I don't know who you are anymore. You're still Mitch, but there's something else."

"I haven't changed."

"Sure you have," she said, a beautiful smile lighting up her face. "You just don't know it yet."

It was at that moment he realized he just might be in love.

THE FIRST THING Bentley saw when she got off the elevator was the room service cart in front of suite 1600. She quickly looked to Mitch. He'd seen it, too.

"Come on," he said. He grabbed her hand once more and pulled her after him as he ran down the hall. The carpet was so cushioned, they barely made a sound.

She had to suppress a wild urge to giggle. She felt like a kid in school, racing with her best friend to snatch a glimpse of the gorgeous and mysterious history teacher. Her heart pumped faster and cleaner, running was easy and fine. She couldn't remember when she'd felt like this. Probably never.

They reached the cart, and Mitch looked at her. She saw the same goofy grin on his face that must have been on hers. He was enjoying this, too. The being together part.

He let go of her hand and put his finger up to his lips. She nodded. No way she was going to spoil this party. The door to 1600 was open, just a bit, but enough for them both to realize it wasn't locked.

Mitch pushed the door slowly open, and she waited for a shout to come from the waiter, or even Colker himself. But it stayed quiet. Too quiet. Her heart pounded loudly in her chest and she had to remind herself that no one else could hear it.

The door moved another inch. Mitch got braver and stuck his head inside. The next second, before she had a chance stop him, he went inside.

She didn't know what to do. Should she go with him? Should she stand guard? The anticipation was too much. The worry—what if Colker had a gun—made it impossible to be still. She looked to the right, then to the left, nearly hopping in her anxiety.

Come on, come on, come on, come on. The chant was a voodoo charm, an incantation that would bring him safely out so they could make their escape.

Come on, come on. Nothing could happen to him. She wouldn't let it. Not now. Not when she'd just—

The door shot open and Mitch burst out, holding something big under his right arm. "Come on!"

She heard herself squeal as she raced after him down the hall, looking back over her shoulder, certain they were going to be caught any second. Instead of waiting for the elevator, Mitch pulled open the stairwell door. She raced in and he followed, and they both collapsed as soon as they were safely inside.

Their breathing echoed off the gray walls, hard and fast and filled with relief. Mitch, still holding his prize, pressed his back against the wall and slid down until he was sitting. She finally realized what he had in his hand. It was a trash basket. Little wadded-up pieces of paper were inside, and some other things she couldn't identify from here.

"Trash? You got his trash?" She started laughing then, and she couldn't have stopped if her life depended on it. Mitch joined in, which made it even funnier, and she had to hold her sides from the ache. She, too, slid down the wall so they were sitting side by side, neither one of them able to stop.

He quit first, but then he looked at her and started again. Then she put on the brakes, only to burst out laughing again at the sight of the trash basket. Now it seemed that she'd finally gotten over the worst of it, although a stray giggle slipped out once or twice.

She took a deep cleansing breath, then dug in her purse for a tissue. Her makeup must be all over her face, and she couldn't find her mirror. She did the best that she could, dabbing underneath her eyes.

When she was through, Mitch reached over and rubbed a spot with his thumb. The gentleness of the touch undid her, and she leaned forward and kissed him.

It wasn't a long kiss. It wasn't terribly passionate. It was simply the best. The best because this guy, this crazy lunatic who'd stolen his way into her life, had somehow stolen his way into her heart.

She pulled back, studying his face, wondering when he'd changed from the Mitch she knew at work to this Mitch.

"Confusing, huh?" he said.

She nodded. "I didn't expect this."

"Me, neither."

"So, what next?"

He smiled. "What say we reconnoiter in our room. Go over the booty."

She nodded. "Good idea."

He stood up first. She took his outstretched hand and let him pull her to her feet. She didn't move, though. She just met his gaze and saw her own wonder reflected in his eyes.

He handed her the trash basket. "You go on to the room," he said. "I've got to run downstairs for a minute."

She took their prize, confused, but not for long. She nodded. "Good idea."

MITCH NEARLY RAN through the lobby toward the gift shop. He couldn't believe he hadn't brought any condoms with him. Well, he had the one in his back pocket, but that was circa 1995. He'd seen several brands behind the counter and thought he just might buy a few of each. They'd be here for another three days, after all.

He barely noticed the hubbub around him. He did see the canvas sheets tied around the front entrance, and he caught the sense of urgency. But he was in a little panic of his own, with no time to worry about anything as minor as a hurricane.

He finally entered the gift shop and saw the neat rows of condoms on the right side of the cash register. Three different kinds should be enough. While he was at it, he picked up some gum, a magazine and some mouthwash.

The girl behind the counter rang up his supplies carefully, perusing each item for the little bar code, then typing the numbers in one by agonizing one.

"Some storm," she said.

"Yep."

"My boyfriend, Eddie? He says the whole island's gonna be ripped up. He says that there won't be anything standing after. I don't think so."

"You're a smart girl."

She smiled but lost her place. Mitch vowed to keep silent.

"This hotel is really big, right? I mean, it would

take a giant hurricane to blow it down. And this one's not even aimed at us. Right?''

He nodded.

She pressed the final button. ''Fourteen fifty-two.''

He gave her fifteen dollars and waited while she struggled with the change.

She put the receipt in the bag and moved to hand it to him, but stopped short. ''Hey, you're that guy Shelli told me about, aren't you?''

''Me?''

The girl nodded. ''Yeah. You're the reporter fellow. Come here to do some big news story.''

''That's right, and I have to go call my editor, so—'' He held out his hand.

She gave him the bag. ''She said you looked like George Clooney, but I don't think so.''

''I'm sure George will be pleased.'' He turned, desperate to make his getaway.

''I didn't mean you weren't cute or anything,'' she called after him.

''Thank you!'' With that, he was away from the gift shop and headed home.

Just after he'd crossed the lobby, someone caught his arm. At first he thought it was the gift shop clerk, ready to tell him just how cute he was, but it was Danny, Bentley's father. Wonderful.

''Hey there,'' Mitch said, trying not to sound as if Dan were the last person on earth he wanted to see. Except for maybe Babs.

''Well, isn't this a nice coincidence,'' Dan said.

"I was just on my way to meet Dinky, and who do I run into?"

Mitch smiled, looked wistfully at the elevator, then back at Danny, who hadn't let go of his arm. In fact, Bentley's father was guiding him to one of the couches lining the walls. Mitch thought about asking why he would want to meet anyone named Dinky, but that could only lead to trouble.

"Is there something I can do for you?" Mitch asked, dreading the answer.

"Sit with me a minute, Carter. Now that we're away from the girls, eh?"

Mitch sat. He couldn't just blow Dan off. And he certainly couldn't tell him why he was so anxious to get upstairs. So he smiled instead.

"I've been meaning to talk to you about Bentley. I would have preferred doing this before you two got married, but now that I've met you, I'm feeling a little easier about things."

"Things?"

Dan nodded. "She's a special girl, Carter. She's been raised carefully. Groomed, if you will. I'm sure you two have talked about her trust fund."

Mitch thought it best to act as though he knew all about it. A real husband would, right? "Of course."

"There's a responsibility that comes along with ten million dollars, son. A heavy responsibility."

Mitch was trying not to choke. Ten million dollars? What the hell was she working at the *Times* for? Was she nuts?

"There are certain philanthropic duties you two will have. It's not always pleasant, but it's part of the Brewster curse." Dan grinned at his little joke, and Mitch thought he might be sick. Just hearing the way Dan said *Brewstah* with that Boston accent, the way he looked at Mitch as though he were sharing the rich man's secret handshake, made him more uneasy than he'd been through this whole charade.

Dan looked for a response, and all Mitch could muster was, "Yes, sir."

"There's the cottage in the Hamptons. The church in the Commons. The hospital—I'm sure Bentley's told you of our work with Boston Memorial."

Mitch nodded.

"Then there's the issue of an heir. I know Mother has gone on about this, but the fact is, you two need to have a son. As soon as you can. The conditions of the trust are very specific, and try as our lawyers might, there's nothing we can do to change it."

Dan sat forward and studied him seriously. "I want my girl to have the kind of life she deserves, Carter. She's not been bred for an ordinary life. Bentley's got a fine pedigree. Just as you have. She's had her fun, now it's time for her to come back to Boston. Have a child. Take her station."

"I don't think she's ready to give up her job, sir. She's very happy at the *Times*."

"That's where you come in. I want you to talk to her, Carter. You seem like a very sensible young man. I'm sure there's a lot you want out of life yourself. It all depends on an heir, you see. A child.''

Mitch did see. He understood now why Bentley had been so upset this morning. And why she'd needed Carter in the first place. He stood up. ''I've got to go upstairs now, sir.''

Dan stood, too, and shook Mitch's hand. ''I've seen the way she looks at you, Carter. She loves you. She'll do what she has to, for you.''

Mitch pulled his hand back, more upset than he cared to admit by this little man-to-man talk. He'd never guessed that becoming Carter would become so complicated. All he'd wanted was the story.

Now, when he'd just realized he'd fallen in love with Bentley, he fully understood that he could never have her. He could never be a Carter. And a Carter was the only man who would do.

Chapter Twelve

Bentley didn't know what to do with herself. She'd thought about undressing, but she didn't want to seem like the whore of Babylon. She'd turned on the television, but after she listened to the hurricane update and figured the hotel wasn't going to be swept away—at least not tonight—she'd turned it off.

The honor bar held her interest for a bit. Particularly the chocolate. And then there was the brushing of the teeth.

Now, a good half hour after Mitch should have been back, she began to worry. Not that anything bad had happened to him—he was the most resourceful person she'd ever met—but that something about Colker had waylaid him.

She didn't want to think about it. She wanted their first time together to be more important than Darren Colker. But just because she'd found herself liking Mitch, it didn't mean he'd become a totally different person. If an opportunity had arisen for Mitch to follow a lead, then that's where he'd be.

Bentley went to the bathroom and brushed her hair again. She could see the bathtub in the mirror. That big old heart-shaped Jacuzzi where she'd first seen Mitch in his birthday suit. God, he was a fine-looking man. She hadn't realized he had a *body* until today. It was his clothes. The bowling shirts from the fifties, the jeans with the holes in the knees, the dressy T-shirt he used for formal occasions. Who would have guessed that beneath all that was a washboard stomach and death-defying shoulders?

Of course she'd also seen another heretofore unnoticed attribute, but she'd think about that later. When he came back. If he came back.

She tossed her brush on the counter, then went back into the bedroom. The wind had picked up again and was rattling the windows. She stared out at the fast-moving clouds rushing past her, and it felt as though time itself were running out.

Where was he? Had the trip to the gift shop given him time to reconsider? Had he remembered who he was with?

Before this weekend, Mitch had told anyone who would listen all about her foibles. He'd laughed at her mania for organization, her files, her emergency supplies. The words "anal retentive" were used in nearly every other sentence. To call them co-workers was stretching things. They were rivals in the true sense of the word. So did this trip to Hawaii change all that?

Or was this just a brief respite in a continuing battle of wills?

She honestly didn't know. He'd found out her biggest secret and used it to get what he wanted. She couldn't afford to forget that, either. It was still possible that he could say something, do something to blow her charade out of the water.

Another thought chilled her. What if he'd found out not just about Carter but about the trust fund? Was it possible all this wasn't about Colker but about money?

No. It couldn't be that. He would have done something, tipped his hand in some way. There had been many opportunities for him to bring up the subject, and he hadn't. He was a good actor, but not that good. If there was one thing she'd learned by being a Brewster, it was how to spot freeloaders. Nothing had set off her radar, and more important, Babs trusted him. No one got past Babs.

Mitch had managed to endear himself to her parents and, she might as well admit it, to her. Shockingly, she actually liked the guy. A lot. Okay, that was true, and it would probably color their relationship from now on. But did she love him?

An hour ago she would have said yes. Now? Could she love a man like Mitch? He was from another world, as foreign to her as the dark side of the moon. She was a Brewster, with all that entailed. Money did strange things to people, and who could say what Mitch would do when he found out who she really was?

She focused again on the outside world. Maybe she was just being paranoid. He'd probably come bursting in any minute, filled with excitement and raring to go. She'd see that look in his eye, and she'd know that none of it mattered, only the two of them and the moment.

As if in punctuation, she heard the key in the lock and turned as Mitch came inside. She smiled just looking at him, until she saw his face.

It wasn't the look she wanted—it was the look she feared.

"Sorry I'm late. I got sidetracked."

Bentley turned to the window quickly, trying hard not to let her hurt show. "No problem."

"I ran into your father in the lobby."

"Oh?" She heard Mitch put his paper bag down.

"We had a little man-to-man talk."

With that, she swung around. "What did he say?"

Mitch had the decency to look embarrassed. "I'm sorry. I didn't realize all the implications. I was after the story. It was never about prying into your life."

"What did he say?" She'd been such a fool. Why hadn't she considered that her parents would take Mitch into their confidence? That they would try to use him to get what they wanted from her?

He walked toward her, but stopped before he could touch her. "He told me about the trust fund."

"And?"

"And about you needing to have a baby."

She crossed her arms to ward off a sudden chill. "That must have been very entertaining. Now you know all the little secrets of the Brewster clan."

"Wait—"

"I'm sure he talked about my responsibilities, right? About my duty to those less fortunate." She walked by him, intending to sit on the bed, but there was no way she could be still. "I'll wager he didn't tell you all of it."

"You don't have to—"

"He probably omitted the part about Mom's spending habits. About the fact that their portion of what Grandad left them is nearly gone. That my part of the trust fund, *if* I get it, will also be used to bail them out. To keep the cottage, to throw the parties, to buy the gowns and the jewels. He didn't mention that, did he?"

Mitch shook his head. "I didn't know."

"Well, now you do. Now you know that any husband of mine will be used for stud services. The rest is immaterial. Oh, they want blue blood, all right, but more important, they want fertility."

"Your father seemed concerned about your happiness, Bentley. It wasn't just about the money."

"I know exactly what my father was concerned with, Mitch."

"Maybe you could talk to them?"

"You think I haven't?" She went to the closet and

pulled a dress off the hanger. "You think I haven't heard about my duty all my life?"

"So tell them to go to hell."

"What?"

"Tell them to go fly a kite. If it's that bad, why stick around?"

She looked at him, so earnest and certain. "It's not that easy."

He came toward her, the sadness in his face just moments ago now changed to righteous indignation. "Why not? You're good at your job. You have your own apartment. You can make out fine."

"And what happens to them if I turn my back?"

"From what I know about Babs, she'll take care of herself."

Bentley shook her head. "You don't understand."

Mitch lost his fierceness, and she wanted him to get it back. She didn't like the way this was going. Not one bit.

"I think I do," he said. "Ten million dollars is a lot of money."

"I don't care about the money."

"No? That makes you pretty damn unique."

"You would do it? Have a baby just to get the money?"

"Damn straight. It wouldn't mean I wouldn't care about the kid. But you can buy a lot of rattles with ten million bucks."

Bentley looked at the dress in her hand. It was a Donna Karan, and it had cost twelve hundred dollars.

Her shoes were Ferragamos, her purse Gucci. Was she really willing to give all that up? Or was she just a younger version of Babs?

"It's not a crime to want it, you know. It doesn't make you a bad person."

"It doesn't make me Saint Joan, either."

Mitch took the dress from her hands and tossed it on the bed. "Who said you have to be a saint? Bet you'll do a lot of good with that trust fund. I can't think of anyone who would be more generous."

She looked into his eyes, but they were blurred from her own tears. "I can't walk away. I've tried. I'm no better than they are."

He pulled her into his arms, and the comfort there was overwhelming. She felt safe for the first time in years. His arms were steady and his chest was strong, and she'd confessed her sins and he still held her tight. The tears that ran down her cheeks were more grateful than sad.

"You're not bad, kiddo. Neither are they. It's just the way of the world. You got the silver spoon when you were born. No shame in that. It's not the money. It's what it does to you."

She sniffed. "What about us?"

He moved his hand so he could touch her under her chin and lift her face to his. "Let's just go on being partners, okay? Let's get this wedding over with, get our prizewinning story. No one said we had to make a decision today, right?"

"This must all seem ludicrous to you," she said. "I know you didn't have anything growing up."

"I had enough." He kissed her lightly on the cheek. "It's all gonna work out for the best," he whispered. "But no matter what, we had a time, right? One hell of a time."

She shuddered lightly, and not from his warm breath on her ear. It was over. He knew it. She knew it. All the magic had been spent, and now the world was black-and-white again. "Yes," she said. "It was the best time I ever had."

He stepped away, and she felt a great rift grow between them. If only...

"We'd better get dressed," he said. "You promised Babs about dinner."

She nodded and took her things into the bathroom. She had the feeling she'd be a while; it was hard to put on makeup when you were crying.

MITCH WAS GLAD they'd made plans with the Brewsters. It would give him a chance to observe the dynamics of the family from his new perspective. He'd pretty much figured that he'd better butt out of her life, but maybe there was still a shot. It was too late for him to be born rich. Too late on the good breeding altogether.

As he sat down next to Bentley at the restaurant, he wondered what Babs and Danny would say if they knew who he really was. That he was a mutt who'd never known his father. Whose mother was a card-carrying alcoholic. Who'd never gone to college but had finagled his way into a job at the *Times*.

He was the kind of person they donated money to. Less fortunate. That was an understatement.

He looked at his menu, vaguely listening to Babs as she went on about the wedding arrangements. If he'd been on his own, he would never have come here. There were way too many items sold at inflated prices. He didn't mind fast food. None of his friends minded fast food. But for the life of him, he couldn't picture Babs and Danny ordering pizza.

Normally, rich people didn't bother him. Actually, he'd always thought if he ever did marry, he'd go looking for a rich woman. Why not? He had a healthy regard for money, and he had no doubts that having some made life a hell of a lot easier.

Now that he was married, for the moment, to Bentley, he wasn't so sure. He'd never understood that having money was a culture, that it changed very fundamental things about a person. It was like a religion, with rituals and cabals the poor slobs of the world couldn't fathom.

Of course Bentley couldn't walk away. It had been selfish of him to even suggest it. He'd been fishing, that's all. Trying a last-ditch effort to see if there was any way they could work things out between them. Not that he wanted to get married or anything, but the thought wasn't as foreign today as it had been yesterday.

Seeing Bentley's tears when he mentioned leaving

it all behind confirmed everything. There was no
chance. Not for him. She needed her life-style, and
she needed a man that would be an asset. Not an
albatross.

It didn't matter that he thought she was the kind
of woman he could spend a lifetime with. When it
came down to brass tacks, it was all very simple.
Because he loved her, he had to leave her be. She
deserved first-rate goods, not a sad mongrel like him.

"Carter?"

He snapped out of his reverie with the feeling that
Bentley had been trying to get his attention for a
while. "Yeah?"

She nodded at the waiter standing by the table. He
hadn't even noticed. "I'll have what she's having,"
Mitch said, pointing his thumb at Bentley.

"Steamed vegetables?"

He made a face. "Whoa. No way." He looked at
her. "I will never understand women." Glancing
quickly at the menu, he ordered a steak, potatoes and
a beer.

"It's no wonder we live so much longer than
men," she said. "Steak is full of—"

"Save it," he said. "I know all about cholesterol
and fat grams and the food pyramid. But if God
didn't want us to eat meat, he wouldn't have invented
serrated knives."

"That's right," Dan said. "See that, Babs? Carter
knows what he's talking about."

"Carter will probably have a coronary bypass,"

Babs said. "If he keeps eating like that, he won't live long enough to see his son graduate from Harvard."

Danny winked at Mitch. "They don't get it, do they? They don't understand that we have different needs."

Mitch glanced at Bentley and saw her lips press tightly together. "You want some wine?"

She shook her head. "No. Thank you."

"Speaking of wine," Babs said, as if the conversation existed only as a lead-in to her favorite topic, "the champagne arrived, but the liquor for the open bars didn't. Now they're saying the roads are washed out between the liquor store and the hotel. I've talked to the general manager, and he can't help. He needs his supplies for the hotel. I say that with the money I'm spending for this week, he should close the bar right now and give me every last drop."

"No!" Mitch said.

"No!" Bentley echoed.

Babs's brows lifted. "Is there something I should know? Are you two budding alcoholics?"

Bentley shook her head. "I just like knowing it's there, Mother. Like a safety net under the tightrope."

"Tightrope? What are you talking about?"

"Nothing."

"You've been quiet all evening. Have you two had a fight?"

"Nope," Mitch said, pitching in with a smile.

"She's just a little tired. That story we've been working on. It's been tough."

"This is no time for work. For heaven's sake, you can play at that job when you get home. This is Stephanie's weekend, or have you forgotten?"

"No, Mother. I haven't forgotten. You're right. I have been spending too much time playing at my job. What can I do to help?"

Babs smiled. It was a smug victory, and Mitch didn't like it.

"You can put all that wonderful energy of yours into finding a way to get your sister here. She's still in Honolulu, and if she doesn't get here soon, I'm going to have my own coronary."

"I'll get on it first thing in the morning," Bentley said. She sounded pleasant, purposeful, almost cheerful.

That was the most worrisome thing of all.

THEY DIDN'T GET BACK to the room until after midnight. Bentley excused herself to go change. When she entered the bathroom, the lights flickered briefly, then went out completely.

"Ouch! Who moved the damn couch?"

She smiled. "You okay?"

"No," Mitch called from the other room. "I'm injured. I need medical attention."

"Call 911."

"I need attention *now*."

"I suppose you'll be wanting to use my flashlight. And my Band-Aids. And my radio."

"Of course. That's why I love you. You're always prepared."

Her smile fell. He was kidding. But she didn't find it funny. Nothing was funny tonight.

"Hello? You still here?"

"I'm here," she called, trying to make her voice sound cheerful and upbeat. "Can you find my suitcase?"

"The flowery one?"

"No, the Vuitton. The one by the TV."

He was quiet for a moment, well, not quiet—he kept bumping around and cursing—but he didn't speak to her. She finished washing her face and groped for a towel. It was darker than she could have imagined, almost painfully dark.

She found the towel, dried off and set a course for the bedroom. Just as she located the door, a blinding light caught her in the eyes and she grimaced. "I see you found the flashlight."

He waved the beam lower, showing her the way out. "Yep. Listen to that wind. I pity the sailors out there."

"The sailors?"

"I knew a sailor once," Mitch said defensively. "Or maybe he just worked at Sea World. I forget."

She followed the light and made it to her bed without mishap. He illuminated the couch for a moment, and she saw that he'd made up his own bed.

"I'll wait till you're settled," he said. "Can't guarantee you'll sleep, though. Not with all this noise."

It was loud. The wind seemed to be searching for crevices and cracks, pulling and tearing at the windows, at the very building itself. She guessed she should have been scared. But a hurricane seemed a small nuisance next to the fact that her whole world was unraveling.

She climbed under the covers, then glanced at the light and shadow of Mitch. She couldn't see him well, mostly just the shape of him. She remembered—was it just last night?—when she'd seen him in silhouette. How she'd thought he was her dream man.

The joke was on her.

Mitch went to the couch, and she heard him hunker down.

"Any last requests?" he asked.

Yes, she thought. *Let it be like it was, for those few minutes this afternoon. Let me pretend that everything will turn out right.* "No. No requests."

The light went out. The darkness was deep and a little frightening. She couldn't tell whether her eyes were open or closed. The wind found a new voice, a moan that shared her loneliness, a cry in the night. She turned over, burying her head in the pillow so he wouldn't hear her cry.

A long time later, or maybe it had only been a

moment, she felt the edge of the bed dip. She froze, waiting, praying.

"Come on," he said. "Scoot over."

She did, her heart beating a rapid pulse, her hopes climbing fast.

He got in bed with her. She felt his whole body right next to hers, touching her side the way his thigh had once touched her thigh.

Then she felt him move, and his hand was on her cheek. He found her lips with his as if he could see through the night.

His kiss was sweet and sad, and when he touched her tear with his thumb, he moaned, and she knew he cried out for her pain, not his own.

She pressed against him, and he moved his hand to her back, exploring, possessing. Then he reached for her breast, and she guided his hand underneath her gown until he found what he was looking for.

His kiss deepened, and she wished she could see him, his face. She needed to know this was real, that it was Mitch, and that he knew it was Bentley.

He pulled back, kissed her neck, then whispered, "Are you sure?"

"Just say you want me. Say you want *me*."

"More than you can ever know, Bentley. My Bentley."

Chapter Thirteen

Bentley felt his hands grip tightly as he turned her toward him. His breathing was rapid—as rapid as hers. She wanted him in a way that was totally new to her. She wanted him for absolution.

He kissed her again, a soul-deep kiss that melted any hesitation that was left. Then, as she was pulling him closer, he hesitated.

"What's wrong?" she said.

"I think we're moving a little too fast here," he said.

"The bag is on the counter. Is that it? The condom?"

He eased to his side but kept his arm around her shoulder. "No, that's not it. Although it kills me to say this, I think we should consider what we're doing."

"What we're not doing is making love," she said, turning to face him. "Why is that?"

"Because I think you'll be sorry."

His voice sounded so certain. "You think...you

think I'm so feebleminded that I can't decide if I should sleep with you? Is that it?''

Just then, the lights came back on. Where it had been too dark only a moment ago, it was now too bright. Too revealing.

"Shut the lights," she said, "please."

He got up, and she closed her eyes to wait until the darkness came once more. She sighed in relief when he turned everything off except the bathroom light. He surprised her then by getting back in bed and not going to the couch.

"Can we start again?" he asked. "I didn't mean that you were unable to make your own decisions. Honest."

"What did you mean?" She moved away from him, to the far side of the bed. It was safer that way.

"Look, kiddo. I don't normally do noble, but when I do, it's for cause."

She scowled, glad that there was just enough light for him to see it.

He moved over. His body touched hers lightly, all the way down her left side. Still, it was enough to make her temperature rise several degrees.

"Off the record, sweetheart. I know I've been a louse. I marched in and botched everything up for you. I know you came here just for your sister's wedding. That Colker wasn't on your agenda. And I also know that by pretending to be Carter, I've upset the apple cart even further. I didn't want to hear that stuff from your dad, but I did. It's done. I just don't want you to hate me later on, when we're both going after the same story, and I'm winning.''

''What makes you think you'll win?''

''That's not the point.''

She softened a bit, hearing what he said. ''You think I'll regret it, huh?''

He nodded.

''That I'll keep thinking you know this big secret, and that I'll resent the fact that you stuck your nose where it didn't belong?''

''Uh-huh.''

''That you found my personal and private papers, and you didn't hesitate to read them, then use the information for your own ends?''

''I think we're pretty clear on that subject.''

''Okay, then. There's a perfectly good solution to the entire problem.''

''I don't think the windows open up here. You'd have to throw me from the roof.''

She smiled. Damn, he could do that to her every time. Take that nice solid anger and make it vanish. ''That's not what I meant, even though your idea does have merit.''

He lay down again, his head squarely on one pillow, hers on the other. Which was very nice, all by itself. ''The solution is that you have to tell me a secret of equal or greater value,'' she said.

''What? Get out of here.''

''Don't tempt me.''

''How do you know I have a secret?''

"Even you can't be as uncomplicated as you'd like people to believe. There are some hidden compartments in there."

"You're giving me too much credit. Maybe I *am* a simple soul. Sleep when I'm tired. Eat when I'm hungry."

"Lie when it suits you?"

"Cute. You're completely mad, but very cute."

She turned her head. Even from this angle, where it was darker, she could see he was smiling at her. Under the covers, she felt his hand on top of hers, and she took it. He squeezed it, and she knew he'd been right. She wasn't ready to make love to him. What she'd wanted was this. This closeness. This friendship. On the other hand...

"Oh, I do have a secret."

"What?"

His expression turned serious. "I stole your last three expense reports and copied them. I'm sorry. I beg you to forgive me."

"Oh, please. I knew that. Accounting knew that. Even Esther in the photocopying room knew that. You think we're all morons?"

"Not *all* of you. But damn. Esther?"

"Come on. Quit dodging the issue. 'Fess up, Slater. I mean it."

He was quiet for a long time. She heard his even breathing, glad for his proximity. It would have been terrible to sleep alone tonight.

"Okay. I stole a car."

"When?"

"Yesterday, what do you think? When I was a teenager, of course."

"Ah. Nope. Try again."

"What? That's a felony."

"You were too young. Doesn't count."

"Since when do we have all these rules?"

"Since you became Carter."

"Oh. Okay."

Again, he was quiet, only this time, she got the feeling he was really trying. She knew so little about his life that whatever he told her was going to shed some much needed light.

While she waited, she listened to the storm. She was glad she was safe and warm and protected. The wind sounded dangerous, and she wondered what kind of havoc it was causing all around the islands. She hoped Stephanie was also safe, and she felt sorry that her sister was alone and not with Jack.

"I almost killed a man once," Mitch said. "How's that for a secret?"

His voice was soft and low, and she knew he was telling her the truth.

"What happened?" she asked, aware that he was slowly pulling his hand away. She gripped it tighter.

"I was seventeen, but I think this one counts. I hadn't seen my mother in a long time. She'd been in detox again, and the foster family I'd been staying with were something out of a Stephen King novel. So social services sent me back home. Well, it wasn't a home. It was a flophouse in downtown L.A. Twenty-five bucks a week. If you didn't pay, they took your front door.''

Bentley kept herself very still. She was afraid that if she moved, he would stop talking, and she had a very strong feeling that this was much more than an idle conversation for him. He was telling her this because he wanted her to know.

''About two weeks later, I heard some bad noises coming from her room. It was late. A guy was there. That wasn't unusual. But I heard her scream. I broke through her door. This guy, this guy with a big tattoo on his back, a picture of a Chinese dragon, was beating her up. He wasn't particular about what he was doing. Just swinging those huge hands and hitting what he could.''

The wind battered so hard at the window, Bentley thought it would break. But she didn't move. Not a muscle.

''I had a baseball bat. Signed by Mickey Mantle. It was probably a fake, but that was okay, 'cause I didn't play baseball. I used it that night, though. I went at him with everything I had. I was pretty big then, too.''

Bentley felt her throat tighten. The urge to cry was heightened by the grip he now had on her hand. Not that it was excruciatingly tight, but that he was so unaware that he was hurting her.

''I just kept hitting him. My mother was screaming, and he was screaming. People were banging on the front door. Finally, my mother, she was so drunk it's amazing she could do anything at all, she grabbed hold of me. I think she'd been calling my name for a long time. She was screaming that it was my father, that he was my father.''

"Oh, God.''

"I don't know if it was true. He got out of there fast, right to the emergency room, I'm sure. The police came, but they didn't arrest me. I moved out the next day and never looked back.''

"So you haven't seen her?''

"Nope. I don't even know if she's alive or not.''

Bentley turned and put her arm over Mitch's chest. He continued to stare straight up into the dark room. "I'm sorry,'' she whispered.

"For what? You didn't do anything.''

She shook him, but just a little. "You know what I mean.''

"Yeah.'' She saw him nod. "I do.''

She put her head down on his chest and, despite the wind outside, heard the beat of his heart, felt each breath. After a while he touched her hair, petting her softly.

"I bet you didn't realize we had so much in common,'' he said.

She laughed. "Yeah. Twins separated at birth.''

"They talked about me for weeks at the country club,'' he said, and she heard humor there, not just pain.

She lifted herself up. "Well, I'd say you did pretty

well for yourself, Mitch Slater. Despite everything.
You're an ace reporter, you work for one of the largest papers in the world."

"I don't have a Pulitzer yet."

"Give it time."

The moon dipped behind a cloud and she couldn't
see him anymore. But she knew he was smiling at
her. The way a friend does. The way a lover smiles.

She dropped back to her side of the bed. Not tonight. Tonight was for sharing in a different way.

A light came on, and she blinked and squinted. It
was the beam from her flashlight. Mitch had it in his
hand, and he was shining it on the wall.

"What are you doing?"

"I want to show you my magic tricks."

"Should I be worried?"

"Nah. They'll dazzle you with their brilliance, but
it won't hurt or anything." He found her hand and
put the flashlight in it. "Shine it against that wall."

She did. She knew he wasn't avoiding a deeper
discussion. He'd told her the truth, and now he was
telling her that he was over it. The episode was in
his past, part of him, but it didn't own him.

His hand went in front of the beam so his shadow
hit the wall.

"Hand shadows?"

"Watch and learn," he said, folding his fingers
together in the traditional duck maneuver. He
quacked twice and showed her the duck's beak open
and close.

"I've never seen anything like it!" she said. "How did you ever come up with that?"

"It's a secret, kid, but someday I might tell you."

Then he moved his fingers into a slightly different pattern, but the shadow was still clearly a duck.

"Guess what it is," he said.

"Another duck. I think this one has arthritis."

"No. It's a goose. Completely different animal."

"Uh-huh."

He changed it once more, but the shadow still looked like a duck.

"Well?"

"A pigeon?"

"Are you blind? That's a cat."

"It is not."

"I should know. It's my hand."

Bentley laughed. "Don't quit your day job."

He harrumphed. "Fat lot you know."

He added two fingers from his other hand and gave the duck ears. "I suppose you're going to say that's a duck?"

"Nope. That's an animal that doesn't exist in nature."

"It's a pony."

"With a beak?"

"That's not a beak."

"I'm not going to argue with you. If you want that to be a pony, fine. It's a pony."

He dropped his hand and turned to her. "Is that

how you argue? Just give in over the pony? I thought you were tougher than that. I'm really disappointed.''

She turned off the flashlight, leaned over, kissed him lightly on the lips and said, ''We can argue later. I've got an hour free after lunch.''

He caught her and kissed her back, and he wasn't fooling around. She thought that maybe it was time for them to take this to the next step, but then he let her go.

''You have sweet dreams,'' he whispered. ''You hear me?''

''Yes, sir.''

She lay down, certain she wouldn't fall asleep soon, not with him so close. But she did.

Mitch watched her for a long time. When he was certain she was asleep, he touched her face with the back of his fingers. Her skin was incredibly smooth, like silk. He'd never done anything half as hard as not making love to her tonight. But he knew that he couldn't keep her as a lover, so he'd have to keep her as a friend.

He fell asleep with his hand upon her hand.

FRIDAY MORNING STARTED with the phone ringing. Mitch stirred awake and picked up the receiver. '''Lo?''

''Carter? Are you still sleeping? It's nearly ten o'clock. Put Bentley on, would you?''

He nudged Bentley until she opened her eyes. ''It's for you,'' he said, handing her the phone.

She didn't sit up, just tucked the phone by her ear. "Yes?"

Mitch climbed out of bed and went to the window. It was daylight, but fierce outside. If anything, the storm had worsened. He found the remote and flipped on the television. He got a station, although the one he'd watched last night was off the air. The reports were similar to the ones he'd heard before. Hurricane Bonnie was rated a two on a scale of five, and Maui was on the far side of the eye. The full brunt of the storm would hit tonight.

He threw the remote on the couch and went to take a shower.

When he emerged, dressed, hungry, ready to rock and roll, she was still on the phone. He listened for a minute but gave it up after he realized she was speaking to a hotel clerk. There was stationery at the desk, and Mitch needed to do some plotting. Time was running out, and so far all they knew was that Colker was in room 1600 using the name Mr. C. And that hadn't been confirmed, even with the bounty from the trash can.

There was every possibility the hotel was going to lose power sometime in the next twenty-four hours. The hotel staff would be in an uproar. Things could get misplaced. People could be confused. He wanted to be ready when that happened.

"That woman should work for the Pentagon," Bentley said, finally heading toward the bathroom, gear in hand.

"Who?"

"My mother, who do you think? She'd be our nation's secret weapon. A hostile country wouldn't stand a chance."

"While this is a delightful conversation, one I'm simply dizzy to continue later, can it and get dressed. We have work to do."

"What is it with this 'we' business. First her, now you. I wish everyone would quit telling me what to do!"

Mitch smiled briefly. "Yes, dear. Go get showered." He turned back to his paper.

She sniffed her ire, then slammed the bathroom door.

He spent the next twenty minutes jotting notes and ideas, none of which had the ring of a winner. He heard Bentley come out.

"I've got some ideas here," he said. "Mostly if the power goes. But I still think we need..." Bentley stood behind him, her delicate scent turning his brain to mush and taking his power of speech.

"Pretend we're thieves?" she said, reading from his notes, her voice this close.

Then he felt her hands on his shoulders, and the inexplicably erotic feel of her breast pressing against the back of his neck as she continued to read.

"I don't want to go to jail over this story, Mitch."

"Uh..."

"And that's out," she said, pointing at the word *hooker*.

She was quiet for a minute, and Mitch reminded himself to breathe again. To swallow. To blink.

"I do like the one where you rappel down to his window from the roof during the hurricane. Practical as always. That's my Mitch."

She stepped away, and he was able to form a coherent thought. "Got any better ideas?"

"Bribes?"

"Good. That's good. Who?"

"How about your friend Shelli?"

He shook his head. "I don't think so."

"So, someone else. Someone in the kitchen?"

He turned, ready to face her now that she was sitting on the couch and not near enough to touch. "The point is, we have to do something. Today."

"Together?"

Mitch shook his head. "Divide and conquer. Let's get out of here, out into the hotel. I'm more creative on my feet. I need to be able to slink into doorways, hide behind palm trees. Use my action decoder ring."

"When should we rendezvous, Mr. Bond?"

"This afternoon. Twoish. In the stairwell?"

She smiled. "Twoish it is. And I bet I come back with a story."

He raised a brow and twirled an invisible mustache. "A friendly wager, eh?"

"Such things have been known to occur."

"And what are we wagering?"

"The byline."

"Whoa," he said, getting serious. "You don't mess around."

She shook her head, picked up her purse and

opened the front door. "I'll see you in the funny papers."

He just had time to think that she looked better in jeans and a silk blouse than most women looked in formal gowns. Then she was gone. And he had work to do.

BENTLEY CAME OUT of the utility room, praying that no one from the housekeeping staff was nearby. She pushed the cleaning cart as quickly as she could to the service elevator and willed the doors to open. They did, and she scooted inside.

The maid's uniform she'd borrowed didn't fit all that well. It was a few sizes too big, and the muted floral material hung unattractively past her knees. The hair net and the hat would camouflage her from the back, but she didn't know what she would do if someone saw her head-on. The thing was to keep her head down. Keep quiet. The real maids weren't due for several hours, but no one should raise a brow over this little change of plans.

She pressed the button for the sixteenth floor, and the elevator lurched upward. It was going to be so fine telling Mitch how clever she'd been. She could already see her byline under the headlines.

No one stopped her on her ascent. At the sixteenth floor, she checked the hallway. It was empty, as it should be. She'd found out the hotel was woefully understaffed because of the weather, and it would have been highly unusual for someone to be up here.

The cart wheel squeaked as she went toward room

1600. Her tennis shoes didn't make a sound. But as she drew closer, she found her pulse jacked up to high gear.

She reached the door and raised her hand to knock.

"Hey, Peter. The maid's here already."

She froze. It was Mitch! She whirled around, ready to brain him.

The look on his face was almost worth having her cover blown. But not quite.

"Ix-nay on the aid-may," she whispered loudly.

He started to laugh, but then Peter came out of the kitchen, and he became instantly serious.

Bentley turned around, desperate to keep her identity hidden from her old friend Peter. How had Mitch gotten to him? And why had he picked that second to open the door?

"That was quick," Peter said. "It's in the bathroom, honey. I broke the big bottle of lotion."

She thought about running away, as fast as she could. But then her beautiful plan for getting to Colker would be ruined. Instead, she turned, pretended to cough and hid her face with her hand. As she went past Mitch, who was still standing at the door, she stepped on his foot. Hard.

Peter was pouring himself a drink, not paying her any attention. She hurried to the bathroom, and just as she went inside, she heard Mitch call out.

"You can mop the kitchen floor when you're done in there, miss."

Chapter Fourteen

Mitch was enjoying himself immensely. Peter had poured him a drink, then gone off to answer the phone, so Mitch was now free to watch Bentley clean the bathroom.

"I think you missed a spot," he said, sipping his Bloody Mary. "By the tub."

She was bent over a mop, her huge dress flopping around her knees and her anger arcing toward him like lightning. "I'm going to get you for this," she whispered. "The UN will have to intercede before I'm through."

He laughed. "What are you going to do, vacuum me to death?"

"You'll beg for mercy."

"Oh, that sounds kinky."

She stopped mopping, wiped a stray wisp of blond hair from her eyes and took a step toward him. "If Peter recognizes me, you're a dead man."

Mitch stepped sideways and looked into the living room. "He's still on the phone. You know, he is a real good-looking guy. You say he offered you a thousand?''

She grabbed the window cleaner and threatened him with it, her fingers looking mighty itchy on the trigger. ''Stop it, you little weasel. I mean it.''

''No, no,'' he said, putting his hands up in mock horror. ''Don't clean me, please!''

She squirted the cleanser at him, but he ducked, only getting a little wet by his left ear. ''Peter's coming,'' he said. ''Hurry.''

She turned to the mirror and squirted a great deal of soap onto it, making sure her back was toward the door. Mitch felt there was no real need to mention that Peter was still on the phone. He hadn't told a total lie. At some point, Peter would come back here.

''Get him away,'' Bentley whispered, her voice urgent even though it was very low. ''Distract him. Let me out of here.''

''But if I do, you'll get to Colker first.''

''Of course I will. So what?''

''It's this byline thing. I'm just not comfortable with—''

''Hey, Carter.''

It was Peter. Mitch and Bentley both froze.

''Yeah?'' Mitch called.

''You ready for another Mary?''

''No thanks,'' he said, smiling. ''I'm in here with the maid. Making sure she doesn't steal anything.''

''Well, when you're through, come on out here.

I've got a story you'll like. Some broad was up here yesterday, a real beauty. I almost had her for lunch.''

Mitch laughed again, louder this time, so Peter would hear him. ''Hold on. We're getting to the good part. She's cleaning the tub.''

Peter's laugh was surprisingly loud, but then he'd been drinking since this morning, if the glasses littering the room were any indication.

''I almost had her for *lunch?*'' Bentley looked wildly around the huge bathroom, then grabbed a bottle of very expensive after-shave. She opened the bottle and turned it over the sink. The odor of the cologne reached Mitch a second later. When it was empty, she went to her cart and pulled out a container of bug spray. She smiled for the first time that afternoon as she poured the contents into its new home. ''I'll give him a story to tell,'' she said.

''Remind me never to tick you off,'' Mitch said. ''You're diabolical.''

She turned to him, her face inexplicably beautiful with her cheeks so red. ''You have no idea.''

Mitch drained his drink. ''Oh, lookee here. Seems I need a refill.''

''You can run, but you can't hide,'' she said as he walked quickly toward the living room.

Once he was a safe distance away, he stopped. ''Don't forget to change the sheets, Gertrude.'' Then he smiled happily for the benefit of his host.

''So I was telling you,'' Peter said, taking Mitch's glass. ''This broad, she came to the room yesterday.

She was asking about my neighbor, too." He paused, looking thoughtfully at Mitch. "You don't know her, do you? Bentley somebody?"

Mitch shook his head. "Nope. Never heard of her."

"Hmm. Well, as I was saying, she came in just when I was expecting a friend. You know—" he winked broadly "—a friend?"

"Sure," Mitch said, nodding. "I got you, buddy."

"But this broad. She was the best-looking babe I'd ever seen out here. I mean it. I figured George had lucked out and hired a beauty queen or something. But she had real class, too. You know?"

"You'd be surprised how well," Mitch said.

"Huh?"

"Nothing. How's that Bloody Mary coming?"

Peter fussed with the drink for a minute, then handed the glass to Mitch. He'd put in a new stalk of celery, too. "Anyway—"

"Hold it a minute, will ya?"

Once again, Peter got that bewildered look on his face.

"I gotta go to the can," Mitch said.

Peter accepted that pronouncement with grace. "Make yourself at home."

Mitch excused himself and went back to the bathroom. Bentley wasn't there. She was in the bedroom, only she wasn't changing the sheets. She was just standing there, staring at the mess in the room. It looked as if Peter had had one hell of a party in there.

He grabbed her arm and pulled her along with him back into the bathroom. Once inside, he shut and locked the door. "Okay," he said. "You win. I'm going to get him to go inside the kitchen. He won't be able to see you leave. So be fast about it, would you?"

"Why would you do that for me?"

"What do you mean?"

"There's gotta be a reason. You wouldn't do it out of the kindness of your heart. Alleged heart, I should say."

He leaned forward quickly and kissed her on the mouth. "Honey, I love you. Don't you know that by now?"

She looked stunned. "Are you kidding?"

He kissed her once more, for good luck. "I'd never kid about a thing like that." He opened the door and looked around. "Two minutes. Then get the hell out of here."

He waited a few seconds, then started to leave, then remembered to turn around and flush the toilet. Then he really did leave, still not certain why he was giving her the chance to escape. Unless, of course, it was true. That he did love Bentley more than he wanted the story.

Oh, damn.

BENTLEY MANAGED TO MAKE it out of Peter's suite, although she couldn't recall how if she had to. Her mind had been in a fog, swirling with the words "I love you."

The kiss had been quick, the situation ludicrous, but when Mitch Slater had said, "I love you," he'd meant it. How she knew that wasn't clear. But she did.

He loved her, and he knew who she was. Who her family was. Now what the heck was she supposed to do?

She stood in the hallway, staring at Peter's door. She wanted to rush back inside and corner Mitch. Make him tell her what he meant. How he meant it. Was it the kind of love she'd heard about? The kind that makes it impossible to live your life without that other person? Or was it the kind of love that simmered over the years, content to exist but go no further?

It seemed like a pretty important question. But if she went back inside that penthouse, both their covers would be blown. Surprisingly, that didn't matter quite as much to her anymore. After all she'd gone through, after all the struggles, she was prepared to throw her Pulitzer out the window. Well, maybe not out the window, but she was willing to put it on the back burner. Which, frankly, scared her to death.

What was happening here? This talk of love— she'd never thought it would hit her, and she would have sworn an affidavit that it wouldn't be with

Mitch. Holy cow. She wasn't in Kansas anymore, that's for sure.

She reached inside the pocket of her dress and pulled out the selection of key cards she'd borrowed. Turning absently to suite 1600, she slipped the first one into the lock. When it didn't work, she tried number two, all the while wondering if she should, in fact, be opening the door across the hall.

Card number ten did the trick. The door swung open, and she pushed her cart inside the suite. Like Peter's, the walls on either side of her were completely made of glass. The furniture was mostly antique, and the art on the walls looked expensive as hell. She noticed the clouds and the wind outside but had no time to gawk. She had no idea where Colker was. He could walk out any second and find her there. So she went over to the counter between the kitchen and the living room. The phone was there, and so were papers, neatly stacked and weighted by a geode. She glanced down and saw the proof they'd been after. Darren Colker had signed the page with a barely legible hand.

Now that she knew, she turned around, went to her cart and wheeled it outside, shutting the door behind her. The truth was, she hadn't thought any further than that. She didn't know what to do or how to get Colker to agree to an interview. It certainly wasn't going to happen while she was disguised as a maid.

She took one more look at 1600, then she wheeled

her cart to the elevator and took the long ride down to the basement. The whole time, all she could think of was Mitch Slater, and how he'd tilted her world.

BENTLEY THREW THE REMOTE control on the bed. It was almost dinnertime, and Mitch hadn't returned. She'd waited till three in the stairwell. When she came back to the room, she'd been bombarded by urgent phone calls from her mother, from Jack, from the wedding coordinator, from her mother again. Stephanie's chances of getting here in time for her wedding were hovering between slim and none, but Babs wasn't about to throw in the towel. The bachelor party would be held that night, even though it had been moved to a lower-level ballroom instead of the patio, where it had been planned.

Mitch was expected to be there, of course. And while he was watching some girl jump out of a cake, she was supposed to be entertaining the female guests who'd made it to the hotel. Oh, boy. They were going to hold the wedding shower in absentia. The gifts would be opened, the punch would be drunk, the finger sandwiches eaten, all without the bride.

Bentley tried to imagine a worse way to spend an evening, but she couldn't.

Dinner was going to be a buffet, then the men and women would go their separate ways. Which was all well and good, except where the hell was Mitch?

She thought of calling Peter's room. But what

would she say? Mitch probably wasn't there anyway. More than likely he was sitting in Darren Colker's penthouse getting the interview of a lifetime. So much for partnerships.

No, that wasn't fair. She'd have done the same thing if the opportunity arose. Despite what had happened this week between them, there was still the competition. That's what made it fun, and she wouldn't want it to disappear. Well, not completely.

She went to the minibar and got another candy bar. It was her second today, which wasn't like her. She was pretty careful about what she ate, unless she was nervous.

And Mitch sure did make her nervous.

She hadn't been able to keep her gaze away from the bed. She was glad that they hadn't made love last night, but she didn't want to get carried away. Friends were good and all that, but frankly, she wanted to get to know Mitch better. Aw heck, who was she kidding? She was ready to jump the boy's bones. Ready, willing and able.

She'd decided, while sitting in the stairwell, that whatever happened, she was prepared to take the plunge. If there wasn't going to be more than a friendship, fine. She was a big girl. Sex wasn't necessarily tied to permanence. If he wanted to leave it at that, she'd smile, salute and carry on.

Although, and this she'd realized in the elevator, if he honestly did just want to be pals, she wasn't at all sure she was going to be okay. The thought of never having this—this crazy, mixed-up adventure—saddened her beyond reason.

She was having the best time of her life. There, she'd admitted the truth. And more than anything, she wanted it to continue back in Los Angeles and for as long as she was able to keep up the pace. Mitch had shown her what was important. The money didn't have to run her life. She could be in control and continue to be the kind of person she wanted to be. Not just what her mother expected.

The door opened, surprising the heck out of her. She hadn't heard his key. He walked in, all smiles, and plopped himself down on the bed. Casually linking his hands behind his head and crossing his ankles, he looked like the picture of pleased-with-himself.

"You got to him, didn't you?" she asked, rising from the couch.

"I didn't say a word."

"But you did. You got him to talk." She crossed to the bed and shoved his legs over to sit down.

"You know what they say about assumption. It makes an—"

"Oh, cut it out. Tell me."

"*We* have an appointment tonight. With Darren Colker himself."

"You're kidding? How?"

Mitch lost his smile. "Boy, a beer would taste really good right now."

"Oh, would it?"

He looked at her with puppy-dog eyes. "I'm too tired to talk *and* get a beer."

She rolled her eyes and went over to the small refrigerator. She got his beer, then went back to the bed, but held the bottle just out of his reach.

"Hey," he said, the second time she pulled it away.

"Promise you'll never, ever try this little trick again?"

He put his hand back behind his head. "I'm not that thirsty."

She opened the bottle and waved it close to his nose. "Mmm. Beer. Cold."

He made one more grab, but she was too quick for him. "Okay, I promise," he said.

She handed him the bottle. "Now, what were you saying?"

Narrowing his eyes, he gave her a reappraising glare. "How did I ever think of you as a pushover?"

"You know what they say about assumptions. They make an ass—"

"Okay, okay. Point made and taken."

"So tell me about Colker."

"He's short, I mean short short. Like four foot eleven short."

"So?"

"He's also old. And he has this hair."

"Hair?"

Mitch nodded as he took another swallow. "Long

hair, in a ponytail. Which wouldn't be so bad, except he's bald on top. It's…"

"Ugly?"

He nodded. "But he didn't run off when he found out I was from the *Times*. He wasn't thrilled about it, but he didn't call the cops."

"So what did you tell him?"

"That we wanted to do a piece on him, that we'd respect his privacy and not say where he was staying—if he'd give us an hour."

"In other words, you blackmailed him."

"Nah. I like to think that I charmed him with my stunning good looks and charisma."

"I like to think I'm Princess Di. That doesn't make it true."

Mitch smiled, and her heart swelled unexpectedly. It was the warmth, the appreciation, she saw on his face when he looked at her that did her in.

"Come here," he said, patting a space close to his chest. "You're too far away."

She scooted up, a little nervous about that other look in his eye—the one that let her know that hormones were at work. "I forgot to tell you," she said. "There's a buffet for the wedding guests tonight. Then a bachelor party for you and a wedding shower for me."

"Uh-huh."

"I mean it," she said, getting goose bumps from the way his hand was exploring her back. "We have to go."

"I see," he said, sitting up so he was very, very close to her. He didn't kiss her lips, opting for a nibble of her neck instead. "How can we go to the parties," he whispered between nips, "when we have the interview at the same time?"

Her eyes had closed by then, and her reason had slipped away in a puddle by the bed. "Parties?" she whispered. "Oh, right there. That makes me crazy."

He'd found her earlobe and was doing very wonderful things to it, things that puckered up her nipples and curled her toes. "Do that again," she said. "That was very, very—"

He kissed her quiet.

For a long time, she floated in his kiss. She tasted him, the hint of beer not at all unpleasant. Her hands found his shirt, and she pulled it up out of his jeans. Then she ran her hands over his chest, marveling at how masculine he felt. And how very feminine that made her feel.

"What time is this buffet thing?" he said, his voice raspy and low.

"Six-thirty."

"It's almost six now."

"Who cares?" She curled her arms around his neck and got down to business. She kissed him with everything she had. All the moves, all the style.

He gave as good as he got, making her bones melt right inside her body. She was still sitting sideways, which made certain activities very difficult, so she pulled away and stood up, ready to sprawl right next to him.

He moved over, then, before she could lie down, he sat up and swung his legs over the bed.

"What?" she asked.

"It's six. We need to get downstairs. The buffet."

"Screw the buffet."

He smiled at her, but there was a sadness there that dampened her enthusiasm.

"You're not going to tell me I'll regret this, are you? Because I won't. Believe me, I won't."

"Maybe I will," he said, his voice serious. He took her hand and pulled her until she was sitting once more. "Maybe I can't deal with it."

"Why?"

"I like you a hell of a lot, Brewster, but I'm not a fool. I know it's the circumstances, the storm, Hawaii that's making this seem like a swell idea. Once we're home…"

"You really think I'm that shallow?"

He shook his head. "I think you're perfect. But I also know that I'm not Carter. I never will be."

"So?"

He kissed her cheek. "Honey, you deserve a Carter. And I know you'll find him."

She stood up, pulling her hand away. "Dammit, Mitch, stop thinking for me. I'm fully capable of making my own decisions. You don't see me deciding things for you, do you?"

"Don't you get it? I'm *not* thinking for you.

Weren't you listening last night when I told that charming little story? Were you paying attention?"

"I heard every word."

"But did you *listen?* We're miles apart, sweetheart. From different galaxies."

"But..." She almost said it, almost said, "You love me," but the words wouldn't come.

"Hey, look. It's going to be a lot more fun working together, isn't it? Now that I know how tough my competition really is, I'm going to have to be on the ball. No slouching."

"Don't be flippant about this," she said, walking over to the closet. "I mean it."

She stared at her clothes, her vision blurred by threatening tears. Then she felt him behind her, and his hands came to rest on her shoulders.

"I've never been more serious," he said. "In a perfect world I think the two of us could have been great together. But it's not like that, is it? You and I have responsibilities, commitments. Life-styles. Once we're away from hurricane central, things will go back to normal. You with your class act, me with my traveling circus. But I'll always remember this."

He lifted her hair behind her right ear and kissed her tenderly on her warm skin. "This will be my memory. The one that will take me through jobs and old age and the whole nine yards. I'll never forget that for a short time, we had the happiest marriage in the world."

That's when she understood. It wasn't that he was

thinking for her. He was telling her that he wouldn't fit in to her life. That he couldn't fit in. And that she'd never fit in to his.

She thought about Babs and Danny, Stephanie and the house in Boston. The trust fund. The cottage in the Hamptons. Maybe Mitch didn't *want* to fit in. He was a free man, the only truly free man she'd ever known. Would he trade that in for a seat at the Boston symphony? Never.

She stepped away from him. Not far, just enough to break contact. Holding her head up and forcing the tears to back off, she reached for her dress. "We'd better get down there," she said. "They're expecting us."

He didn't move for a minute. Then he turned and walked away.

Chapter Fifteen

Mitch walked into the Lanai room expecting to have a lousy time. He didn't want to be here, he didn't know the groom, he wasn't even part of the family. If these people knew who he really was, they'd either ask him to bus the tables or just plain tell him to leave.

But Bentley needed him to make a good impression, and that's what he was going to do.

It was a small crowd. Well taken care of, though, by some rather lovely ladies wearing wraparound skirts and bikini tops. God bless the USA, Mitch thought. The land of the free and the home of bikini tops.

Big buffet tables lined the walls, and the food rested in canoes. Babs was a creative thinker, all right. She also seemed to have solved the liquor problem, because the two bars were stocked for the coming millennium.

The only person he knew was Dan Brewster, who stood between two big guys with good tans. Before he could face that, he went to the bar and ordered himself a bourbon.

After taking a shuddering gulp, he turned to Danny, who welcomed him with a bonhomie that suggested too much alcohol or nerves, maybe both.

"It's about time you met your future brother-in-law, Carter." He looked at one of the tall men, a big, strapping guy with movie-idol looks. "Jack, this is Carter DeHaven, Bentley's husband."

Mitch took the hand that was extended, expecting the macho squeeze routine, but got a firm yet friendly handshake instead.

"So you're the one who caught Bentley," Jack said with a hint of admiration. "Good for you. She's a remarkable girl."

Mitch smiled. "I think so, too."

"Jack is an Amazon guide," Danny said. "Really. And so's his friend, Rik."

Mitch shook hands with the other man, surprised at their profession. Amazon guide? Wasn't that a bit like being an astronaut or a treasure hunter—jobs that existed only in books and movies?

If he'd felt out of place before, it was only a rehearsal for the way he felt now. Not only was he not able to compete moneywise, he didn't have nearly enough testosterone to be a part of this clan. He would have felt better if he'd never met Jack or his friend. They both looked more like Carter than he ever could, and he was sure if he stuck around, these two would catch on.

"So you work for CNN?" Jack asked. "I know some people there. What division?"

"News. Background news. Research."

Jack nodded. "So you do know Cary."

Mitch nodded, wondering if Cary was male or female. "Good old Cary."

Jack's brow went up. "When I worked with him, there was nothing good about him."

"I don't like to tell tales out of school," Mitch said, planning his escape. He had two objectives: get out of here before his ruse was discovered, and get up to the sixteenth floor for the interview with Colker. There was only one thing to do. He gauged his timing, and when Danny went to welcome another guest, Mitch stepped in as if he'd been bumped and poured his glass of bourbon down his shirt.

"Oh, I'm sorry," Danny said. "I didn't realize you were standing there."

"It's okay," Mitch said as the three-piece band started playing "Huki-lau." He pulled the sticky wet shirt away from his skin. "I'll just run upstairs to change."

Before he could move, there was a commotion at one of the doors. Mitch watched as a giant wedding cake was rolled in, and he cursed his timing once again. There were few things in life as entertaining as a giant wedding cake. He'd learned that early and well.

But Danny handed him a wad of napkins to clean the bourbon off his shirt, and then the lights flickered once, twice, then died completely. It was pitch-black in the room, but the band kept playing. A chorus of disappointed moans contrasted with the plink-plink of the ukulele.

"I'll go get candles," Mitch said. "Hold tight."

He only bumped into four people and two tables as he floundered toward the door. Once he was outside the ballroom and the door was shut behind him, he reached into his pocket and pulled out the key-fob flashlight. It was small but powerful, and he could just make his way toward the lobby.

The wind howled against the tarps, threatening to break through, drowning any hope of conversation. But the staff was on the ball. Candles were already lit on most available counters. He grabbed one and shielded the flame as he hurried toward the small room where Bentley was showering the absent bride.

It was surprisingly easy to find her. She was standing in the hallway with a flashlight in her hand.

"I'll never make fun of your safety precautions again," he said. "You ready?"

"To climb sixteen floors?"

He nodded. "You're in pretty good shape. I'll pull when you get tired."

"Okay. But how are we going to conduct the interview in the dark?"

Mitch patted his coat pocket. "You're not the only Girl Scout around here. I've got my tape recorder."

"Ah, Mitch. I'm so proud of you. I'm also amazed that you can stand. Whoa, that is some smell."

"Yeah, well, it was my way of wishing Jack a happy wedding."

"Dousing yourself in liquor?"

"Don't ask. Let's get going."

She led him to the stairwell. Just before they entered, he blew out his candle. No need to worry about that now. He could light it again once they were with Colker.

IT TOOK QUITE A WHILE to climb the stairs. They kept meeting people along the way, some going up, some down. All of them seemed to be in very chipper moods. And friendly. Very friendly.

Bentley wished Jean and Ruth, the latest in a long string of new best friends, good-luck and continued climbing. Only two more flights and they would be home free. Mitch was beside her now, and she could hear his harsh but steady breathing. She'd surprised herself with her stamina. All that stair climbing at the gym had finally paid off.

When they got to the sixteenth-floor stairwell, they rested a moment. She smiled. "We just worked off an apple," she said.

"What?"

She watched the bouncing circle of light from her flashlight. Every time she breathed, it jiggled, and she was breathing hard. "That climb. It burned off the calories of an apple."

"That's it? An apple? I think it was more like all the moon pies I ate when I was eleven."

"Nope. Trust me on this. I know."

"I grant you all the calorie wisdom," he said. "You ready for the interview?"

"As I'll ever be."

He opened the door, and she pointed her light down the hallway. It was dark, so dark, and quiet. She couldn't hear the wind from here, but once they were inside the suite, they'd have a bird's-eye view of Hurricane Bonnie. She realized her quickened pulse wasn't just a result of her climb. She was excited. Excited to see the storm, to meet Colker, to get the interview of a lifetime. To do it all with Mitch.

They reached 1602, and she was grateful Peter's door was closed. Mitch knocked at 1600, then pounded on the door. No Colker.

"Maybe he can't hear you," she said.

He banged again, then tried the door. It opened. She shined the light in Mitch's face, and his look of surprise matched her own.

"Should we?"

"We have an invitation," he said.

They walked inside, moving slowly. Bentley used the flashlight to skim the room. It was loud in here. Scary, too. All the windows rattled, and she could just imagine them popping, one after another. Something big struck and she jumped, but nothing broke.

"Mr. Colker?" Mitch took out his little flashlight and joined in the search. "It's Mitch Slater. From the *Times*."

It was clear Colker wasn't in the living room. Mitch signaled her and they went to the kitchen, then the bedroom. The decor was fabulous. She wondered if Colker had used his own decorator or if this was what the hotel provided.

"He's not here," she said, only she had to yell to be heard.

"I can't imagine where he'd be," Mitch said, also shouting. "He knew we were coming."

"We didn't try the bathroom."

He nodded and led her to the master suite bath. It was very large, and the Jacuzzi tub was big enough to hold four. Even there, the sounds of the storm frightened her. The world was blowing away, and she could swear she felt the building sway.

"He's gone," Mitch said. "We'll wait."

She nodded. They went back to the living room, and she walked toward the windows, mesmerized by the sharp prattle of rain on the glass.

"Don't get too close there," Mitch said. He grabbed her arm and pulled her back just as something huge crashed into the lowest pane on the right and shattered the glass.

It sounded like an explosion, a huge crash that tore a hole in the sky. She felt the spray hit her, and wondered if it was just rain or shards of glass.

"Come on," Mitch said, pulling her toward the bedroom. "Let's take cover."

"Wait," she yelled. "His things will be ruined if we don't cover that hole."

"It's too dangerous."

"Help me move the couch." She turned the flashlight on a love seat.

She put the flashlight on the end table, the beam pointing straight up. It gave just enough light for them to do the job. She took one end of the sofa, he took the other, and they moved it against the hole in the window.

It didn't completely block it off, but it helped. As she went to get the flashlight, she kicked something hard. It was a coconut. That's what had broken the glass.

Something new crashed against the window. The pane held, but Mitch grabbed her and pulled her behind him. "We're leaving. Now!"

He hurried her in the bedroom, but there was a big window on the right side, so he continued to pull her into the bathroom. Once inside, he shut the door, and the sound of the storm diminished sharply.

"I can't believe this," she said. "Are we safe in here?"

Mitch nodded. "I think so. Geez. Can you imagine what's happening in the bad part of this hurricane? That's some nasty wind."

Bentley took the candle out of his hand and set it on the counter. He handed her a matchbook, and she lit the wick. Then she set up her flashlight so it shone in the mirror and reflected back. The bathroom was actually kind of romantic, and if she'd been alone, she would have drawn herself a bath on the spot.

"So how long do these things last?" Mitch asked.

She turned to see him sitting by the tub. "I don't know. Maybe the whole night."

"You think Colker is safe?"

She shrugged and sat down beside Mitch. "Maybe he was in the elevator. I imagine there had to be some people stuck there." A thought struck and she stood up. "My mother. I think she's on the elevator."

"Why?"

"She went upstairs just before the power went out. She went to find Tildy."

"Well, if she is in the elevator, there's nothing we can do about it."

"Can't you climb down the shaft? Open the trap door?"

"Unfortunately, I left my Superman cape in my other suitcase."

"It shouldn't be that tricky. Don't you think we should try?"

"Sit down, Bentley. I'm sure your mother can take care of herself. The safest thing for us to do right now is stay put."

She did sit, but her worry didn't diminish. "I wonder if she's in there alone. Or if someone got stuck with her."

"Babs is a very resourceful woman. If there is someone with her, I'm sure they're glad she's there."

Bentley giggled. "Yeah, I'll bet."

"Hey, I'm sure she's calm and quiet, the picture of patience."

Bentley laughed out loud. "That's only if she brought her tranquilizers with her."

He reached over and rubbed her back, making her feel instantly better. "Tell you what. Let's not talk about Mom for a minute."

"What do you want to talk about?"

His kiss answered her question. She leaned into his arms, feeling his heat go from zero to sixty in two seconds. Hers wasn't far behind.

It was awkward, sitting on the edge of the tub, angled toward each other, and Mitch stood, pulling her up with him. After one more kiss, he broke away.

"Hold that thought," he said. He grabbed the flashlight and went into the bedroom. She paced, waiting, wondering if she should talk to him about this afternoon. If she should tell him that it just might be possible that she loved him. Would that make things better? Or worse?

He was gone long enough for her to have thoroughly confused herself. Each decision was scary, and a satisfactory resolution seemed just beyond her grasp. If this was ever to work, one of them would have to give up a life they'd grown used to, and she didn't know if she was strong enough. Or if he would ever want to.

On the other hand, maybe there was no decision to be made. How could she trust her feelings about Mitch? Everything she'd known about him before

Wednesday was awful. He'd tricked his way into stories that rightfully belonged to others. He'd never had a relationship that lasted more than a week. If you needed someone to count on, it wouldn't be Mitch.

So how come he'd been so wonderful to her? How come he'd turned her universe upside down and sideways? Had she been with the *real* Slater? Was all that rumor and innuendo just rumor and innuendo?

He walked back inside carrying an armload of pillows and blankets. Smart boy. She grabbed a few things from the top. "Great idea."

"I told you I wasn't just pretty."

She smiled. That was true. He had told her there was more to him than his looks or his reputation.

He'd dumped his pile of linens next to the tub, then he began to build a nest inside it. Pillows, blankets, layers of soft, cozy comfort. She handed him her stack, and then it was done. A perfect place to ride out the storm. Warm. Close. Intimate.

Mitch put the flashlight back on the counter, locked the bathroom door, then turned to Bentley. "After you," he said.

She started to climb into the tub, but stopped to take off her heels. Then she did get in and lay down, feeling very much like a pearl inside an oyster.

The tub was long enough for her to stretch out all the way. Even Mitch would only have to tuck a little. She watched him take off his coat and his shoes. He hooked one leg over the edge, then paused. "I can get the flashlight. You didn't see all my shadow puppets.''

"A person can only stand so much greatness," she said.

He nodded. "Right." Then he climbed in and settled down next to her, their bodies touching from toe to shoulder.

"Lean forward," he said. She obeyed and his arm went in back of her neck. She curled toward him, putting her arm across his chest and her leg across his legs. She'd never been more comfortable—except for the odor of bourbon—and not because of the pillows.

"Thank you," she whispered.

"For what?"

"For everything. For sticking your nose in where it didn't belong. For stealing Carter. For lousing up my life."

"Stop, you're making me blush."

"There's one thing, though."

He rubbed her cheek with his thumb. "What's that?"

"This." She moved over and kissed him, and it wasn't a gee-I-want-this-to-be-platonic kiss. It wasn't that at all.

While she kissed him, she unbuttoned his shirt.

He pulled back a bit, lifting her chin so he could meet her gaze. "Do you know what you're doing?"

She nodded. "It smells really bad."

"I don't mean that. I mean—you won't regret it?"

"I'll regret it if we don't."

"But…"

She moved her hand from his shirt to his face, tracing his lips with her finger. "Don't you get it?" she said. "I love you, kid."

She heard his sharp intake of breath. "It's not that easy, snookems. There's the whole situation with your—"

"Mitch?"

"Yeah?"

"Shut up."

His sigh fanned his sweet breath across her cheek. Then he came closer, and this time, when he kissed her, there was a joy, an urgency, a surrender that hadn't been there before.

Now that she knew it was real, and that he wanted her as much as she wanted him, she couldn't wait. She got on her knees to pull his shirt from his pants, which wasn't so easy because he was trying to reach behind her to unzip her dress at the same time.

She realized she was smiling, that her pulse was racing and her heart was pounding from excitement. She'd always thought of making love as a solemn event, with lots of serious gazes and heartfelt sighs. What she couldn't wait to find out was what making love with Mitch would be like.

It wouldn't be ordinary, that's for sure. Not solemn, either. With Mitch, it would be a trip to the moon.

She got his pants unzipped with no calamitous

mistakes, and he stood up to take them off. It was hard for him to balance, and when she stood, she could see why. Although the nest was comfy, it wasn't very stable.

His pant leg got caught on his ankle and he hopped several times trying to disengage it. Bentley couldn't help but laugh.

"Bentley, honey," he said. "Off the record, laughing when a guy takes off his pants isn't the way to make friends and influence people."

"Then a guy shouldn't get his pants caught on his foot."

He yanked the pants free and tossed them aside. "Voilà."

Although a lot of him was in shadow, several important features weren't. She could see, quite plainly, that he was excited, too.

She quickly pulled her dress over her head, grateful that she managed it without getting stuck. Then he started laughing.

"Doesn't that laughing business go for the girl, too?"

He pointed to the wall beside him. "Look. There's a shadow I've never tried before."

She turned and saw a rather large bulge in the shorts region, clearly visible against the wall. His laughter made it kind of bounce up and down. She pointed. "It's a duck!"

He shook his head. "No way, doll. That's a pony."

She lost it. She tried to get her panties off, but she couldn't do it. Finally, she turned her back to him, determined to get it together. It took a minute, but she did it. Her bra followed her panties over the side of the tub to a pile on the floor.

When she turned back, she saw he'd also removed the rest of his clothes. She wished like hell that the lights would come back on. She wanted to see his body, not the way she had the other day, but now, when he was wanting her so plainly.

"Come here," he said, holding out his arms.

She did. The feel of him naked against her body was enough to chase all her giggles away. Every part of her was ready. Her nipples were hard, her breasts full. Her readiness didn't stop there.

When he brought his hand down, slowly down from her breast to her stomach, then further, and inside, she was ready there, too.

She kissed his chest once, twice, then echoed his movements until she gripped him, hard and full, in her hand.

He moved her quickly, urgently, until her back was against the cold tile wall. She gasped, but soon that didn't matter. He surrounded her with his arms, pushed her legs apart with his leg. His face was all in shadow, but when he paused, she knew he was asking her, one final time, if this was what she wanted.

She reached for him once more and brought him inside her. "Yes," she said.

Chapter Sixteen

The earth moved. Really.

Mitch felt the whole damn building rock, and he wouldn't have been a bit surprised if they left this little love nest and found out the hurricane had been gone for hours.

"You should really think of doing this professionally," he said as soon as he had his breath back. "I mean it. We're talking Nobel prize here."

"Thank you," she said. "I think."

"For a minute there I heard harps," he said, stroking Bentley's cheek. "Did you hear harps?"

She chuckled and he felt it all the way through him, what with her head resting on his chest. Her arm was around his waist, her leg curved protectively over his legs. The pillows were soft, the flickering candle danced against the mirror, and he'd never been more content. Never.

"I think that was me you heard. Gasping. I mean, three times? That's some stamina there, bucko."

"Give me a minute and a transfusion, and I'll be ready again."

She coughed. "Right. Gee, you think we should leave a nice thank-you note for Mr. Colker?"

He laughed. "How would you word that exactly?"

"I'll look it up in my Emily Post."

"You know what would be good right now?"

"Hmm?"

"A beer."

"And some bagels."

"Apple pie."

"No. Cheesecake."

"Women and cheesecake. I don't get that."

"It's the texture."

"*This* is texture," he said, running his hand up her arm, then segueing to her chest and her breast. He cupped her in his hand, marveled at the delicate skin, the still-hard nub of her nipple, and thanked God again for making him a heterosexual male.

"What time is it, do you think?" she asked, her voice all throaty.

"I don't know. I don't care."

"What if Colker comes back?"

"He can't come in."

"It's his suite."

"He still can't come in."

"And we aren't going to leave?"

He shook his head, feeling the soft pillows cushion him on each side.

"Nope. We're going to stay like this forever. Except we'll call room service."

"Interesting plan."

"I can't see any downside."

She tucked her hand underneath him, tightening her embrace. "I wish it could last," she said.

He heard a hint of sadness there, a slice of cold reality. He wasn't ready. "Hey, no fair being logical."

"One of us should be."

"Then let me do it."

"Why?"

"Because I never let logic get in the way of fun. It's part of my personal credo."

He actually felt her smile against his chest.

"What's the rest of it?"

"I don't believe there's a story I can't get, I don't believe I'm paid nearly what I'm worth, and I don't believe in lite beer."

"That's some credo."

"It's gotten me through some very tough times."

Bentley didn't say anything for a while. He felt her warm breath on his skin, and when he touched her arm he noticed she had goose bumps. He searched blindly for a blanket and found one, then tossed it over them. "You cold?"

She nodded. The feeling of her in the dark, speaking to him with her body, was maybe the most wonderful thing he'd ever known. He didn't want to give it up. Not now, not ever. She felt right. Perfect.

"I hate to say it," she said, "but I think we should get up and find out what's going on out there."

"Oh, now there you go. I told you—"

She lifted her head. "Mitch. It's time."

He nodded. She was right. It was time to go back to the real world. Back to being partners, rivals, friends. Why the hell did reality have to be so damn cruel?

She started to lift up, but he held her still for a moment. He needed to say this in the dark, where she couldn't see his face. "I have to tell you something," he said.

He felt her tense. "Go ahead."

"I never want to hurt you," he said, picking his words carefully. "I never want to embarrass you or make you cry. I think you're the most courageous person I know. And for the record, I don't give a damn if I never get the Colker interview. I'm just grateful that I got to be Carter for a while—"

She jerked away, struggling to stand. He wasn't sure what he'd said to upset her. He'd tried so hard to be nice. "Bentley?"

"Shut up, Mitch," she said.

He could hear she was crying. Great, he'd blown it in one hot second. "I didn't mean—"

"I said, shut up." She climbed out of the tub and grabbed her clothes.

He could see her half in shadow and half in light, and he realized all over again how much he'd come to love her. But he didn't fully know her. He'd need a lifetime for that.

She sniffed, and then he heard her zip up her dress. He wanted to comfort her, but he'd already botched that job. Feeling cold now himself, he got up and climbed out of the tub.

"I'm going to the living room," she said. "I need to see."

"I'll be right out."

"Can you do this if I take the flashlight?"

He nodded. "I want to strip the pillows and stuff."

"I'll wait for you out there." She grabbed hold of the flashlight, the beam jerking as if she were trembling. Then she left the one spot on earth where she'd really been his.

BENTLEY SAW that hours had gone by. The night that had brought her so much was being torn apart by the sun. The wind still howled, but now she knew it was rage that spurred it on. Her rage matched it blow for blow.

Why? Why did it have to be so perfect? And why could it never be again?

She wiped her face with the back of her hand. She told herself to grow up, to face this like an adult. It probably wasn't even love. It was a crush, or a fixation, and those didn't last, did they? But were crushes supposed to hurt like this? Maybe that's where they got the name. They crushed the life out of you and made you want to scream.

She went to the window, not caring one bit that something could shatter the glass. Pressing her face against the cold pane, she felt the fury of the struggle just inches away. She knew just what it felt like to get battered and pounded.

She'd give it all up. The hell with the money. Her family would simply have to learn to live like everyone else. Babs could learn to cut coupons. Shop at bargain stores. Buy her clothes at secondhand stores. And so could she, dammit. Anything. She'd do anything, if only she could make it work.

A shuddering gust swept the glass and took her foolishness away with it. He would never believe that she wanted him more than the ten million dollars. If she took the money, he would leave. If she didn't take it, he would send her away.

"Hey, get away from that glass. Are you crazy?"

She turned, and the light was enough for her to see him across the room. "It's calming down, I think."

"There's still no power. But the water is running."

"Good. I want to go to our room. Take a shower."

He walked toward her, holding the flickering candle in front of him. "Are you okay?"

She smiled brightly, as only a Brewster could. "Of course. Let's go."

"Should we leave a note for Colker?"

"I think it'll be okay. We'll catch up to him later."

He stared at her for a long while, and she knew he was trying to think of something comforting to say.

She walked to him, touched his cheek with the back of her hand. It was coarse with a night's beard, yet achingly soft. "Please don't think this is your doing," she said. "I just don't have a wonderful credo like you. It's the logic that does me in, every time. That pure, awful logic."

He wrapped his arms around her, careful of the candle. He hugged her tight, rocking her back and forth. "I can't think of a way out of this one, snookems. I wish I could."

She nodded once against his chest, and she resented his shirt for being in the way. "Ironic, huh?"

"God save me from irony. That's the other half of my credo."

"I wish I could laugh," she said. "I wish one damn thing was funny right now."

"Well, there is your mother in the elevator."

She smiled. How could she help it? He undid her with his voice, with his wit. So close. They'd been so very close. "There is that. I bet she's opened the doors with her bare hands."

"I wouldn't doubt it for a moment."

Feeling stronger, at least for now, she left his embrace. It was still too dark to see the fine lines in his face, the nuances that could tell her so much. Was he hurting as deeply as she? Was he still thinking about their differences, instead of how very much they were alike?

He turned away from her abruptly. As if he'd known she was trying to discover his secrets. "Wonder if Darren has a cold one in this place."

His voice sounded strained. But he'd shown her one thing—they had to get on with it. Get on with the wedding, even though it would kill her that it was her sister getting married and not her. But then she remembered it was Saturday already. Stephanie could never get here in time.

"We have some beer in the honor bar downstairs," she said. "But I don't know how cold it'll be. The power's been off all night."

"I won't like it, but I'll drink it."

"Good man," she said, aware as she spoke how feeble the joke was. But it was the best she could do.

He blew out the candle and left it on the coffee table. Then he took her hand and led her to the door. She looked back once, trying to see the tub, but of course, she couldn't.

IT WAS DURING HER SHOWER that she made up her mind. Now, taking a cold, hard look at herself in the bathroom mirror, she knew she had no choice.

She snapped her compact closed and went to the bedroom. Mitch was waiting for his turn in the shower. He looked so wonderfully at home among her things. He was on the couch, thumbing through her issue of *Vogue*—barefoot, shirtless, his hair tousled and his chin dark with the beginning of a beard. She wanted to make love to him right then. The ache was more than physical, and she wondered if that ache was going to be a part of her from now on, like her hair or her fingers.

"It's all yours," she said, trying to keep her voice cheerful. That was another thing she suspected would last long past this trip. Forcing herself to sound chipper, to put on a happy face.

He tossed the magazine aside and smiled up at her. She saw her own bittersweet emotions echoed on his face. That same effort to look like all was right in a world gone terribly wrong.

"You leave any hot water?"

"That's the one thing we've been left with," she said. "I really do want to get downstairs and see what happened during the night. I wonder if the tarps held?"

"I'll hurry," he said, standing. He walked by her and touched her briefly on the arm. "Have some juice. The kitchen probably won't be open."

She nodded absently, not caring whether she ate or drank. She wanted to get out of here, find her parents, get on with it. If she lingered too long, there was a chance she'd change her mind.

Today was supposed to have been Stephanie's wedding. Of course, without the bride, there wouldn't be a ceremony. Her whole trip had been for nothing. No wedding, no story. She would have been better off staying at home. God, she wanted to get back there as soon as possible.

Was the airport even open? She went to the window and saw that while it wasn't anything like last night, there was still some serious wind out there. A palm tree she'd barely noticed before made her look twice. It had been snapped in two. Bentley sent up a small prayer that no one had been hurt, that no one's life had been taken.

Then she turned back and went to the closet. She chose jeans and a T-shirt instead of the cream-colored suit she'd planned on wearing for today's activities. She might be asked to help, and she wanted to pitch in.

Mitch came out of the shower just after she'd put on her sneakers. He was clean shaven once more, his hair wet and spiky. He'd wrapped a towel around his waist.

"That felt great," he said. "I see you decided to dress like the common folk."

The comment stung. "What the heck," she said. "I'll try to blend in."

"Hey, I didn't mean anything by that. Honest."

She knew he hadn't consciously meant to hurt her. But the blatant reminder of their different worlds had hit her like a blow.

"Where do you live?" she asked.

"Echo Park."

"An apartment? A house?"

"Apartment. Duplex, actually."

"What does it look like?"

He shrugged as he pulled a clean pair of jeans from his duffel bag. "Nothing special. Salvation Army furniture. Brick-and-wood bookcases. Posters on the wall."

"No pets?"

"Not even a plant. I'm not home enough to take care of a pet. Not the way a pet should be taken care of."

"Do you stick things on your refrigerator?"

He smiled. "Yeah, I do."

"I do, too," she said, excited for no logical reason. "I use little magnets and I stick pictures and articles and ticket stubs on there."

"Did you hear? There's a new children's museum downtown," he said, grinning. "All the artwork is hung on refrigerators."

She laughed, but the humor drained out of her quickly. "It's silly, isn't it? Tacking things up with a magnet. It doesn't matter at all."

She could see he was searching for something to say, but she hadn't meant to put him on the spot. This was her own private battle, and there was no need for him to get hit by the shrapnel. "Come on, get dressed already. Don't you want to hear how Babs spent the night?"

He nodded, but she could see he was worried. Soon he would know that he needn't be concerned about her.

Mitch dropped his towel, and her cheeks flushed

at his casual nakedness. There was no reason for modesty anymore. Not after last night. Still, it was an intimacy she no longer deserved, and she picked up the *Vogue* and tried to focus on the pictures.

"I'm ready if you are," he said after a few minutes.

It was safe to look up again, and she did, pasting her smile on as if donning a hat. "Great. Let's hit it."

He held out his hand for her. She stared at it, completely choked up by the small courtesy. But the smile didn't waver. Not a centimeter. She took his hand, and he helped her up. Neither of them spoke, although they stood very close to each other. She could smell his clean scent, feel his body heat. She stepped away.

MITCH CURSED HIMSELF for a fool. He should comfort her, make her see that things weren't so terrible. Once she got back to L.A., she'd remember who he was. She'd see him in context, and she'd wonder how she ever let herself get so crazy over a poor slob like him. Maybe she'd look back with kindness. He hoped so. He hated to think she would have regrets. He would, but not about what had happened, only about what hadn't.

They walked down the stairs, crowded with guests, most of them looking worse for wear. He doubted anyone had slept last night.

When they reached the lobby, he was relieved to

see that the tarps had held. Nothing looked too bad inside, just a few broken vases, a tipped palm tree or two. The place was packed with people. Children slept on the couches, though, so it was remarkably silent. Trust a hurricane to make people considerate.

"I don't see anyone we know," Bentley said. "Wait, there's Kimo." She rushed over to the exhausted-looking bellman. "Can you tell me where the Brewster party is?"

He looked at her for a moment, as if trying to remember who she was. "Oh. In the Lanai ballroom. Most everyone slept there last night."

"Babs Brewster?"

His face got that exasperated look Mitch had come to associate with those who had encountered Babs. "She's fine. We got her out of the elevator early this morning. She's back there with the rest of them."

Bentley nodded knowingly. "I'm sorry."

"You didn't do anything."

"But she did. Guilt by association."

Kimo smiled. "She's really something."

Bentley nodded. "Let me know if there's any way I can help out today. I'm going to check up on her, but I'll come back if you need me."

He shook his head. "We won't be able to do much until the wind dies down some more. The cleanup is going to be mostly outside."

"The offer stands," she said.

Mitch felt proud, which seemed a bizarre thing to feel. Why should he puff up like a peacock because

Bentley offered to help out? It must be the lack of sleep.

They threaded their way through the crowd. Mitch barely noticed anyone; his gaze was fixed on Bentley. She walked so straight and tall. With such natural grace. Although he was glad that he'd seen her nude, with all the trappings of wealth stripped away, it saddened him, too. She had a richness about her that had nothing to do with wealth, and everything to do with wealth. Her lithe body moved with stunning ease and self-assurance. He wondered if she'd studied ballet or attended a finishing school.

Bentley led him inside the ballroom where the bachelor party had been the night before. Babs was holding court, a bevy of wedding guests standing at her feet with deep sympathy etched in every pair of eyes.

"Where have you been?" Babs called when she caught sight of them. She made a beeline for Bentley, nearly pushing Tildy off balance. "You don't know what I've been through. It's been hell. I tell you, Bentley, you have no idea."

"I'm sorry the hurricane inconvenienced you, Mother."

Babs stopped short, her hands still extended for the aborted hug. "What's the matter?"

Bentley took a deep breath. She straightened her already straight back and pushed her hair from her face. "I have something to tell you," she said.

"It can't wait? I've not slept at all. Daddy got drunk last night, and he has a deadly hangover."

"No, it can't wait. But you probably should hear this privately. Daddy, too."

Babs looked at Mitch questioningly. He shrugged and shook his head, but he had a terrible feeling he knew what Bentley was going to say. He couldn't let her. Not this way. It was all his fault.

"Excuse us a minute, Mom," he said as he turned to face Bentley. "What are you doing?" he said softly. "Are you crazy? You don't have to tell them. I'll never let on. I'll be Carter whenever you need me to."

Bentley shook her head. "No. This isn't about you, Mitch. It's about me. About who I am. And what lies I'm willing to live with."

"If I hadn't been here…"

"If you hadn't been here, I'd probably have gone on telling my parents what they wanted to hear. I would have bent my life around to fit their mold. And little by little, I'd have died inside. Don't you dare feel bad, Mitch. You make me brave. How I'll be brave without you, I don't know. But I'll try."

He swallowed hard. "What are you telling me? That you're going to give up the money?"

She shook her head. "I don't know. Maybe. I'll have to wait and see how things turn out. What I won't do is compromise for one more day. I won't hide anymore. For the first time in my life, it *is* my life, and I'm not at all sure how I want to spend it."

"The Pulitzer?"

She nodded. "I'll still beat you to that prize, kiddo. Or my name isn't—"

"Bentley Brewster-DeHaven," he said, loud enough for Babs, for all of them to hear. He turned around and met Babs's gaze. "You wanted a wedding. You're going to get a wedding." He took Bentley's hand in his, ignoring the shocked look on her face. "We're going to renew our vows. Today. Right now. There's got to be a preacher here somewhere."

Babs smiled brightly, her immediate woes chased away by the thought that her expensive wedding wouldn't go to waste after all. "This is wonderful," she said. "Danny, did you hear? We're finally going to see Bentley and Carter get married."

Mitch felt Bentley tug at him until she finally yanked him around.

"What are you doing?"

"Getting married."

"Are you crazy?"

"Hey, I'll change my name. I've come to like Carter. He and I share the same taste in women."

"You can't do this."

"Why not? We've pulled off harder things than this. Listen, it wouldn't so bad, would it? I'd leave you alone, I promise. It would kill me, but I'd leave you alone."

She looked up at him with eyes brimming with tears. "No, you don't understand. I don't want you to change your name or anything else. I'm doing this because I need to. Because I want to. Because I love you.''

"You do? For real? It's me here, Bentley. Mitch, not Carter. I'm from the poor side of town, kiddo. I've been on my own for a lot of years. I'm no piece of cake.''

"You think I am? I don't give a damn about the money, Mitch, but it's there, and we'll have to deal with it. It can change people, you know. It might change me.''

His heart was beating a mile a minute. "I'm willing to take that risk. Are you?''

The tears had broken free and were trickling down her cheeks. He kissed them away, and then she whispered, "Yes.''

Chapter Seventeen

"But it has to be my way," Bentley said. "No more lies."

Mitch nodded, his smile so gentle and loving that she knew nothing could hurt her. She kissed him lightly on the lips and turned to face her parents.

"Mother, this isn't Carter."

Babs blinked several times. Her smile still played on her lips, but now it looked painful. Despite her makeup, Bentley watched her pale. "What?"

"This isn't Carter. His name is Mitchell Andrew Slater, and he's a reporter for the *Times*."

"What have you done with Carter?"

Bentley walked over to her mother and took her hands. "There never was a Carter, Mom. I made him up so that you would stop sending me potential husbands. I realize I should never have done that. It wasn't fair. I should have told you a long time ago how I really felt."

"I don't know how to react to this, Bentley. I'm at a loss for words. You made up your husband? All this time, you've been lying to me? To your father? My God, what will I tell people? How am I going to explain this?''

''I hope you're going to tell them that your daughter made a mistake. But she never stopped loving you, or respecting you. And now you're very happy for her. Happy that she's found the man she wants to spend the rest of her life with.''

Babs took her hands away. She looked as though she might cry, but that wouldn't happen. Babs never cried.

''How can I be happy for you? I don't know this young man at all. Who are his people? What can he offer you?''

''I don't have people, Mrs. Brewster,'' Mitch said. ''It's just me. All I can offer your daughter is everything I've got. Which isn't a whole hell of a lot, but what I lack in goods, I make up for in sincerity.''

Bentley took his hand in hers. ''I'm crazy about him, Mom. And you will be, too. He's just what this family needed. A man who wears a bowling shirt to his own wedding.''

''You're serious about this?'' Babs said. ''Danny, talk to her.''

Dan nodded and walked up to Bentley. He took hold of her shoulders and settled his gaze point-blank. ''You really love him?''

Bentley nodded.

''Can you live without him?''

''I probably can. But I don't want to.''

"You know he loves you?"

"Yes."

"Then you have my blessings. I still want that grandchild, though."

"We'll do our best, Dad."

"Danny!"

He turned to his wife. "What is it?"

"I thought you were going to talk her out of this. You know she's a special young lady and that she has certain needs."

"Beulah Brewster, you listen to me. Our daughter is a grown woman. She's capable of making her own decisions. She's done nothing but make us proud, and I don't see that this will turn out any differently. Now, you wanted to throw a wedding. So kiss your new son-in-law and get on with it."

Babs's mouth hung open in total surprise. "We'll talk about this later, Danforth."

"I know we will, dear." He kissed her on the lips. "And I know you're going to make the best of things. You always do. That's one of the reasons I love you."

She didn't look happy, but it didn't look like she was going to fight them any longer.

Bentley had never been so proud of her father. Or felt so dearly for her mother. It was as if the dust of years had been blown away, and now she could see her parents with all their faults and love them completely.

Mitch put his arm around her waist and whispered, "Beulah?"

She laughed. "I warn you. This is not an easy family. Are you sure you're up for this?"

"Let's find us a justice of the peace and snookems, I'm all yours."

She turned to him. "One promise?"

He nodded solemnly.

"Never call me snookems again."

"Spoilsport."

"Promise?"

He nodded. "Boy, I propose in this idyllic setting, I dress up in my best clothes, and this is what I get in return?"

"Quit complaining and find us a preacher before I decide I need a real wedding dress."

"Anyone here who can officiate a wedding?" he shouted.

The milling guests were looking on as if watching an episode of *Dallas*. From the very back, a small voice cried, "I can."

Bentley tried to see who it was. Finally, a man stepped forward. A short, short man, bald on top, a long ponytail in back.

She turned to Mitch. His mouth was open, so she knew that it really was Darren Colker.

"What are you doing here?" Mitch said.

"I'm here for the wedding."

"For my sister's wedding?" Bentley said, utterly confused.

"Bentley," Babs said, "this is your father's old friend. Surely you've heard us mention Dinky."

"*This* is Dinky? Darren Colker is Dad's old college roommate?"

Babs nodded. "Of course."

"Why didn't you tell me?"

"You never asked."

"So do you two want to get married?" Colker asked. "Or do we want to discuss the old days at Harvard."

"Are you allowed to do that?" Bentley said. "Marry us?"

"I'm a minister, and I can officiate anywhere in the United States."

"What about our interview?" Mitch asked.

Colker, the strange-looking little billionaire, stared up at Mitch and Bentley. "Ah, now there's the rub. You want to get married, or you want an interview?"

"Both is probably out of the question," Mitch said. "Right?"

Colker nodded.

"Then get ready, Mr. Colker. 'Cause we're having ourselves a Hawaiian wedding."

BENTLEY STARED at the ring on her finger. As things would have it, that was what she'd borrowed. The fake flowers she'd lifted from a hotel vase were something old, her jeans were something blue, and her name, Bentley Slater was her something new. All in all, no wedding had ever been more perfect.

"The elevator still isn't working," Mitch said. "And if I'm not mistaken, we're officially on our honeymoon."

"That is a problem."

"Shall we walk?"

"I say we run."

He grinned, and she knew she wanted to see that smile for the rest of her life. She'd never been more hopeful, more content, more excited. All from Mitch Slater. The last man in the world she would have figured. Just last week, she would have crossed the street if she'd seen him coming. Now she never wanted to leave his side.

"If I get tired, will you carry me?" she asked.

His grin turned devilish. "Only if you give me that kickback story you've been working on."

"You've got to be kidding," she said. "*Give* you my story? I married you. I didn't get a lobotomy."

They entered the stairwell, and his laughter echoed off the walls.

She sighed. Life was certainly going to be interesting from now on. And if they didn't end up killing each other, it was going to be more fun than she'd ever known.

"I guess that means I won't be sharing the Hardesty story with you," he said as they started their ascent.

"You don't have anything on Hardesty."

"No?"

"What? Tell me."

He picked up the pace. "Nope. I didn't get a lobotomy, either."

She ran faster until she was able to grab the back of his shirt and get him to stop. He turned around, his face very serious but his eyes filled with mischief.

"You *don't* have anything on Hardesty."

"I could have."

She crossed her arms.

"All right. *We* could have. See, I have this theory—"

She shook her head and held up her hands. "Just this once, what do you say we don't use journalism as foreplay?"

He pondered for a moment, then stepped down to be right next to her. "Okay. Just this once. But I know you love it."

"Yeah," she said, letting her sarcasm match the moment. "Newspaper lingo makes me hot."

He leaned over so his mouth was very close to her ear. "Copyedits," he whispered. "Lead-in. Byline."

She pushed him away, laughing, but he captured her hands in his. Then he did the very best thing he could have. He kissed his wife.

And the adventure began.

Epilogue

One year and four months later...

"Listen, honey," Mitch said, pulling out an office chair and giving Bentley a smile of overblown sympathy. "You shouldn't be rushing around after a gangster like Pelby. He's too dangerous. It wouldn't be safe for—" Mitch reached over and put his hand on Bentley's rounded belly "—for little Carter."

"You're right," she said, smiling as sweetly as Miss Congeniality herself. "That's the thing I love about you, Mitch. You're so considerate."

He cast his gaze down demurely. "I love you, sweetheart. That's all."

Bentley kept her smile in place while Mitch sidled over to his desk. He picked up his tape recorder and slipped it in his back pocket, as nonchalant as you please. Her blissed-out grin didn't waver as he eyed the folded paper where she'd written Pelby's address. Pelby was ready to talk, to implicate his own men in one of the largest black market rings in the country. The story had Pulitzer written all over it.

"I'll be back before you know it," Mitch said. "You just take it easy, you hear?" He started toward her desk, moving slowly and stealthily, backing away from Bentley and her smile. "Don't forget to take your vitamins. I've got the beeper, so if anything should happen, I'll be back in a flash."

"Okay, honey. You be care—" She froze and put her hand on her stomach. A scared grimace took the place of her smile, and she reached out wildly with her left hand in her attempt to find the chair.

"What?"

Mitch was beside her now, the address forgotten in his concern. His gaze went back and forth between her belly and her face. He knew full well that she was only seven months along.

"What is it?" he said. "A contraction? You're not supposed to— It's too—"

"Uh..." She grabbed onto the chair and leaned against it heavily. "Maybe some water," she said, her voice cracking in pain.

"Should I call an ambulance?"

She shook her head. "No. Just the water. Please."

He nodded, panic-stricken, and ran out of the room.

Bentley smiled again and stood up straight. As quick as a wink she grabbed her own tape recorder and snatched the address from the desk. Then she hurried, as fast as a pregnant lady could, to the elevator.

Mitch raced back to the office as she entered the elevator, and turned just as she pressed the Down button.

"Wait," he yelled, racing toward her. "Where are you going?"

The doors began to close. "To do *my* interview."

"But...but the contractions."

"Contractions? Who said anything about contractions?"

"Why you—"

"Bye, darling. I'll see you tonight. Kiss, kiss."

The door closed, and Bentley laughed aloud. After all this time, Mitch still didn't stand a chance. Poor baby. She'd have to be extra nice to him tonight. Not that it would be hard. She was crazy about the guy. She closed her eyes, sending up another quick thank-you to the man upstairs. "For everything," she whispered.

The elevator stopped at the first floor, and the doors whispered open. Bentley stepped out at the exact second Mitch crashed through the staircase door. He stood in front of her, panting. "Oh, no you don't, Mrs. Slater."

"No?"

He shook his head. "Not without me." Then he smiled at her. The grin was filled with mischief, excitement and, oh, so much love. What could a girl do? She covered the two steps that separated them, grabbed him around the neck and kissed him.

Of course, while she was at it, she reached down to his back pocket and slipped his tape recorder out. This was her story, after all, and no matter how great his kisses were, he wasn't going to steal it.

Mitch kissed her back, loving her more than life itself. She was everything to him. She and, soon, little Carter. It was hard to believe, but even the trust fund hadn't knocked them off course. Who knew love could be this good? Or why he'd been so incredibly lucky?

Of course, none of that stopped him from reaching down to her purse and pilfering Pelby's address. No matter how fantastic her kisses were, this *was* going to be a joint-byline story.

She just didn't know it yet.

COMING NEXT MONTH

#697 SPUR-OF-THE-MOMENT MARRIAGE by Cathy Gillen Thacker
Wild West Weddings

Cowboy counselor Cisco Kidd never expected to be a fifteen-minute fiancé in a client's matchmaking plans. His intended, Gillian Taylor, was certainly anxious to say "I do." While her sexy sass turned on his every desire, her eyes held secrets—secrets he'd spend their required honeymoon seducing from her.

#698 PLEASE SAY "I DO" by Karen Toller Whittenburg
Three Weddings & a Hurricane

Rik Austin wouldn't let wedding planner Hallie Bernhardt disrupt his plans to disrupt this wedding. He knew just what to do—a little tequila here, a little seduction there. Before she knew it, Hallie would be bewitched and bewildered—and the wedding would be history. But a funny thing happened on the way to disaster....

#699 VERDICT: PARENTHOOD by Jule McBride
Big Apple Babies

Overnight, the "Sexiest Man in Manhattan," Grantham Hale, became the adoptive daddy of quadruplets *and* twins! But his real troubles start when the quads' presumed-dead—but very much alive—biological mother reappears and the judge sentences Phoebe and Grantham to be parents... together!

#700 MR. WRONG! by Mary Anne Wilson

Guardian angel Angelina had worked hard to turn Melanie Clark into the proper mate for "Mr. Perfect." But *now* Angelina finds out Melanie is destined for Mr. Perfect's rougher, tougher, untamed brother...a guy Melanie can recognize at forty paces as Mr. Wrong!

AVAILABLE THIS MONTH:

#693 MISSION: MOTHERHOOD
Jule McBride

#694 BOSS MAN
Linda Cajio

#695 QUICK, FIND A RING!
Jo Leigh

#696 A RELUCTANT ROGUE
Pam McCutcheon

Look us up on-line at: http://www.romance.net

Everyone loves the *Holidays*...

Four sexy guys with two things in common:
the Holiday name and humbug in the heart!

PETER

the holiday heart

MICHAEL

by Linda Cajio

This year Cupid and his romantic cohorts are
working double—make that quadruple—time, not only
Valentine's Day but also Mother's Day, Labor Day and
Christmas—every holiday season throughout 1997.

Don't miss any of these heartfelt romances in:

May—#678 BACHELOR DADDY

September—#694 BOSS MAN

November—#704 MISTER CHRISTMAS

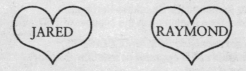

JARED

RAYMOND

Only from Harlequin American Romance.

HARLEQUIN WOMEN KNOW ROMANCE WHEN THEY SEE IT.

And they'll see it on **ROMANCE CLASSICS**, the new 24-hour TV channel devoted to romantic movies and original programs like the special **Romantically Speaking-Harlequin® Goes Prime Time.**

Romantically Speaking-Harlequin® Goes Prime Time introduces you to many of your favorite romance authors in a program developed exclusively for Harlequin® readers.

Watch for **Romantically Speaking-Harlequin® Goes Prime Time** beginning in the summer of 1997.

If you're not receiving ROMANCE CLASSICS, call your local cable operator or satellite provider and ask for it today!

Escape to the network of your dreams.

Harlequin American Romance
cordially invites you to

Three Weddings & A HURRICANE

AT THE PARADISE HOTEL
MAUI, HAWAII
(Weather permitting)

with a special appearance by Hurricane Bonnie

❦

Three couples + one hurricane =
lots of romance!

Don't miss this exciting new series blowing your
way from American Romance:

#691 MARRY ME, BABY
by Debbi Rawlins (August 1997)

#695 QUICK, FIND A RING!
by Jo Leigh (September 1997)

#698 PLEASE SAY "I DO"
by Karen Toller Whittenburg (October 1997)

Available wherever Harlequin books are sold.